GETTING IT WRONG
WITH
UNCLE TOM

By the same author

GETTING IT WRONG
WITH
UNCLE TOM

A Norfolk Idyll

David Holbrook

GETTING IT WRONG WITH UNCLE TOM

First published in 1998 by
Mousehold Press,
Victoria Cottage,
Constitution Opening
Norwich, NR3 4BD

Cover design by Terry Loan

Illustrations by David Holbrook

ISBN 1 874739 09 9

Printed by Watkiss Studios Ltd, Biggleswade

For Jonny and Thomas

Uncle Tom's

ONE

I had never stayed away from home before. When I opened my eyes, it took me a long time to think where I was. Above my head was a frame of black metal rods with brass knobs on. I lifted up my head, and against my chin was a heavy, mealy white bedspread lying very cold and clean over me. The pillow was big and hard, and the room was bare, except for one wooden chair and a wash-stand, and a dim picture showing a woman in a bonnet feeding some ducks.

I was on old Isaac Walker's farm! My Mum had said they get up ever so early on farms, so I slid out of bed quick, and started to pick up my clothes and pull them on. After I got my trousers and shirt on I poured a bit of cold water out of the big jug into a basin, and splashed my face with it. Then I washed my hands a bit with the bar of green soap and dried myself on the white towel. I opened the door a bit and listened, thinking what I ought to do. Outside the window the sun was beginning to shine on the heavy swathes of foliage on the trees at the end of Bayfield Park. I could see the park gates along Cley Road from Letheringsett. Across the road the cornfields spread away to the woods, the barley in them turned whitish yellow. I was on the farm! I wanted to get out in the open. So I overcame my shyness and groped my way down the stairs.

I came down to a door through which I could hear the noise of feet, tea-cups, voices and the clatter of pans.

I knocked, a bit timid.

'Is that Duffy?' said a voice in a Norfolk accent, with its rising singsong. 'Is that boy Duffy? Come you on in, boy – why, you're ready dressed then? Blast, he's off, Father, in't he?'

Old Mrs Walker had a big red face, browned by the sun, that was, with little wrinkles and veins all over it. She talked all the time and every word she said she rolled her eyes, or screwed them up, or put up her eyebrows, or pouted or smiled at you, so as to make her meaning more plain. Only I could never take my eyes off her face, that kept time with everything she said. And while she was talking and mimicking at you with her face, she would be doing things with

1

her hands, too, arranging knives and forks or wringing out the wiping up cloths she called a 'dwile' or setting the kettle properly on the hob, or tucking bills behind the clock: she was an active old body, like some kind of automatic doll in a museum wound up and going when you put a penny in, and that talk of hers just set off and never stopped.

Her old man, Father Isaac, used to have to shut her up to get a word in.

'Now what would you like to eat my little man,' she set off. I hated being called 'little man': I was fourteen after all. 'Would you like a sausage or a slice of farm bacon or some baked beans or a slice of fried bread or you can have an ornery hen's egg or a duck's egg, and there might even be a goose egg if Donald hain't et 'em all …?'

I didn't know what to say, and when I was thunderstruck like that by her flow of talk, old Isaac used to say 'Ha!' and chuckle to himself, as if to say 'you see what I have to put up with, crackin' her jaw night and mornin', don't you take no notice'.

'Bacon and hen's egg, please,' I managed to get out at last.

So I sat down, and started on a big plate of bacon and egg Mrs Isaacs frizzled up in a big black iron pan. She put that down on the table covered with oilcloth, along with a big piece of bread, and a cup of tea. That was thick and reddy brown with cream and sugar in it. The kitchen was a big room all full of odds and ends. That smelt of cattle cake, a kind of sweet corny smell, rubber boots and paraffin: there was farm rubbish everywhere, all jumbled up with the pots and pans and food, and everything.

'He's a peaky-lookin' little old bugger,' said the farmer, grinning at me, with his pipe pulled out a little way. His teeth were stained brown and green, with big grooves across them. I couldn't understand what he was chuckling about: he seemed to think I was a great joke, and this upset me. I didn't know how to take him and I was a bit worried because I was going to stay with him for three weeks.

As he went on teasing me I looked around at the muddle everywhere: there were guns and gloves and bundles of binder twine, sacks, jars of tar, and all sorts of farm stuff. Mrs Walker she had a little old basket of new-hatched goslings by the coal fire range, and two puppies whining and scuffling in a cardboard box alongside it. I wasn't to touch them she said: but I could look at 'em.

Old Mrs Isaac, she was real broad Norfolk. When she wasn't

talking at me, she was grumbling and grunting to herself, and the embarrassing thing was that she seemed to think I was about seven or eight, rather than fourteen. She'd never had any children, and I suppose that all came out in her, to be motherly. Anyway, she started 'little mannin'' me as soon as I got into the house, and all this stuff about were my 'dannies' clean and did I like 'cushies', and that. I didn't know where to look when she went on like that. She had this nice smile and she kept nodding at me, but she was so anxious to please I got afraid she would eat me. She was a big, plump woman with black hair in a bun and she wore big flowery print frocks that made her look bigger. Her pinafore today was covered with yellow sunflowers. I felt if I didn't look out she'd smother me before I got through the time of my stay.

I don't think she ever thought about what I was feeling because she went on huckering to herself all the time, whether I was there or not. When I realised this I felt much better because I could see she lived in a world of her own and it was better not to take any notice. She lived in a sort of fantasy she made up. It didn't matter whether old Isaac was there or 'the men' or me, or just the goslings: she went on mobbing and mobbing to the mealy air of that old kitchen of hers, to the goslings or the dog or the pigs, or just the bags of hen pellets. Old Isaac never took any notice of her.

'Now my little man,' she'd say. 'Just hull me over the dwile agin. One of them little old goslin's have done suffin on the tiles. So I better tricolate that up all round here. Old Isaac he'll start a-huckerin' about me this mornin' 'cause I've got to wash over the kitchen floor an' set the stool's foot in water, well, never mind, I aren't one o' them datty mawthers never was I never balk at any datty job not me like old Mrs Liddamore, blast when she'd finished her tea she'd hull all the muck up the back stock 'stead o' coppin' that out in the yard. Everythin' in her kitchen was as black as hakes ... Blast that was like Pockthorpe!'

I couldn't understand half of it. Her talk was full of characters no one had ever heard of: Mabel Liddamore and 'Mother', and Aunt Agnes who was struck by lightnin' and had her arm twisted right round so that bent the other way. And she'd go out in the yard, and talk to the bullocks and pigs as if they were human. The little pigs turned their trough over that morning and she say, 'You naughta bors, you been a-routin'. I shall ha' to put a ring through your snouts we don't want none o' your chelp. Look, Duffy, they keep a-tryin' to

3

crowd underneath the fence. Where do you think you're goin' together? Git back in there. I'll give you what for! They're right shy wanakin' little devils they are ... I shall hev to make yew inta pork pies!'

She went on like that all the time.

There was another lodger in the house and that was Donald their tractor driver. He came back in from milking and sat silently for his breakfast. He was a thin, sallow man of about twenty with a sad face and he just sat thinking all the time, blinking his eyes.

'Go you and sit down bor,' said Mrs Walker to him, 'I'm now a-comin' wi' your breakfast. If I'd a known you'd bin goin' to come just now I'd a-had that ready. Now I've got to be a-goin' out to see them men a-feedin' them hens 'cause they never do nothin' right.'

A man they called old Abbs come to the door for the farmer, and she tut-tutted to him: 'Old Isaac he just now went through the pightle a seein' if he can't get a rabbit but he in't far away 'cause I heard him a-hollerin' th' old dawg not a minute ago. If I han't had this here mash to make for the goslin's I'd a-gone after him for you. Hold you on, he's now a-comin'.'

And all the time she was steaming backwards and forwards with old saucepans full of meal or bits of toast or cups of tea, or jugs of milk, mixing and stirring, cutting and slapping things on plates for me and Donald.

'Is that old boy behavin' his self?' asked old Abbs about me.

'He han't had no chance to do anything else yet,' said Donald sadly. 'He's only just got out o' bed and had his breakfast.'

That set old Mrs Walker off.

'Well, when Mr Ransome handed him over he said, "Do you make him do as you do, don't he en't do right." Of course, he say, "If he don't do what you want him to do, I don't want you to do anything to him." If he don't do as he ought to do, though, what kin I do? Any old how, if he start a-puttin' on his parts he on't get nawthen, that's sartain.'

She didn't mean no harm, I could see, because when she said that she came out of her dream and give me a fat old smile and a nod, and another piece o' toast, and old Abbs he wheezed and grunted: they made a good pair. Donald had put his bacon and toast away as if by magic and he was into his overalls, and off. I followed him quick, before old Mrs started on me again.

That sunshine was so bright I couldn't see nothing for a bit.

4

Then I could see that 'the men', as Mrs Isaac called them, were putting together a trailer to get the harvest in. There was this big old fat bloke called Abbs and a very bent, little, wiry old man called Charlie Bacon and old Isaac the farmer in charge, and me. Donald went off horse-raking a field that had already been cut, to drag up the odd bits of barley. Old Isaac he went off and left me with 'the men' or 'the boys' as Mrs called them – though one of 'em was near eighty, I thought. Old Abbs he was a wheezy old fellow, with fat cheeks and great big hands like a bunch of bananas, and greasy dark grey trousers. He was a bit bald, with stringy grey hair and a big long nose like a pale carrot. But you could see he was all right because his face was all creased up in a smiley sort of way. I couldn't make him out at first because he made out he was being stern and bossy, but that was all squit, really. He talked through his nose with a whirr and wheeze, like an old chapel harmonium what's got a stop gone wrong and stuck out all the time.

'Hum ... ha ... hum,' he said. 'Blast, Charlie, we shall be all right ... hum ... now we've got young Samson here.'

Old Charlie Bacon chuckled. He was the one nearly eighty.

'He look as though he've bin shut in a cupboard for six months. What do they feed you on, bor?'

'Smitticks and suslams ... hum ...' said old Abbs wheezin'. 'He look right crawly-mawly dorn't he! Don't you just stand there a-gawpin' boy, or we'll all get the sack. See if you can push that there eujackapivvy through that there hole while we lift up this here end. Hum ... umh ... hum.'

'Are you ready ... hum? ... Now!'

I pushed on the large steel bolt he'd shown me and, luckily, suddenly it slid in between the two eyes on the trailer and the eye on the tractor. Then old Abbs fixed it with a split pin, while Charlie and I did up the tail boards.

'Blast, he' ha' got some strength, you can see that.'

'Tha's only he don't look very fierce.'

All the time they kept chipping me about my strength. They didn't mean no harm, but that made my arms and legs go all like they were made of wool. I had to use a brace and screwdriver bit to drive in some big screws all along the angle iron holding the platform planks together. But that old bit, that slipped and trembled, and I kept puffing and grumbling at it, and that made them laugh.

'You don't have to blow them in you know, bor,' Charlie said.

5

'Blast you make more noise nor old Abbs here, and you can hear his tissack over to Blakeney Point!'

Old Abbs wheezed and coughed. Then he had to spit.

'Blast, he gasp so much, don't you think we could run the troshin' machine off him. Hum ... ha ... urgh.' He spat, the gob going like a bullet into a nettle bed. When the day was ended I was goin' to practise doing that, I thought.

'Or a windmill,' said Charlie, 'for dryin' the corn when tha's claggy! Ho! Ho!'

Old Bacon, he had a leathery brown face all wrinkled up like a crocodile. He had bright blue eyes and he moved his old grey head about like a bird. He put his old neck down to me, and he said 'How old do you reckon I am boy?'

I didn't know what to say. If I said he was a hundred he might think I was being saucy; if I said fifty he'd think I was stupid. So I said sixty and he danced about a bit as pleased as a little boy, so that was all right.

'I'm eighty-vor,' he said. 'Eighty-vor! And I can keep up with the mawthers an' all,' he said.

'That he can,' said old Abbs. 'Ho! Hum ... You see him now, them old gals are comin' down the lane on their old bikes!'

Two girls were riding down past the farm with upright black bicycles with string skirt guards on the back wheels. The old man danced about and waved his arms, a loony kind of smile on his face, his eyebrows right up high.

'Hallo there my beauties,' he cried. 'I'll be arter you ... How about comin' up Petticoot Loke wi' me? Heh, heh, heh!'

'You're old enough to know better, you old fule,' one of the women shouted.

'Ah hah!' he cried, mopping his head with a red handkerchief. I couldn't think what all the fuss was about. Old Charlie Bacon was always like that. He was always showing how lively he was. I thought perhaps he knew he was going to die soon, so he was putting it off as long as he could. Old Abbs kept wheezing and wheezing, and spitting and spitting. Sometimes he would go right out of control, and gasp and spit, choking and heaving as if he was going to have a fit.

'Yew want to go with them old Burnham Market mawthers, boy,' Charlie said to me. 'They're the bors!'

'Oh, Christ, boy, I sh'll die afore this job's done, that old bor's

6

such a blurry specimen,' said old Abbs. 'Here, do you hold that …
hum … eujackapivvy again, then this here'll be ready to goo at last.
Hough! Phut!' And another gob sailed off into the nettles. The trailer
was finished, and now we could cut and cart the next field of barley.

That afternoon Charlie showed me how to set up the sheaves
of corn. We were going to do a big field among the woods on the left
of the road going towards Glandford. Abbs and Charlie cut a kind
of path from the gate all around the edge of the field of barley. They
did this with the scythes, swinging away out of sight along the
hedge, first thing. Later in the morning, once the sun had dried the
field a bit, the binder came in, clattering behind a tractor. That was
a fair-sized field, about twenty acres, between plantations of fine big
trees, with copses of big shady trees here and there in the field. A
binder had a kind of windmill to push the corn against the knife, a
long series of sharp, triangular teeth rattling back and forth along the
cutting edge, so the corn falls on a belt of canvas moving across and
round and round. That looked a right ramshackle effort to me, only
that seemed to work. The cut cornstalks are shuffled into a sheaf, tied
up with the twine and dropped off. Binders are always going wrong.
Charlie told me you have to watch that they were knotting properly.
They'd have to sharpen the knife twice a day, and were always
mending the machinery with bolts and wire. Sometimes the drive
from the tractor power shaft broke when the 'eujackapivvy' sheared,
said Abbs, so we had to work a new bolt in.

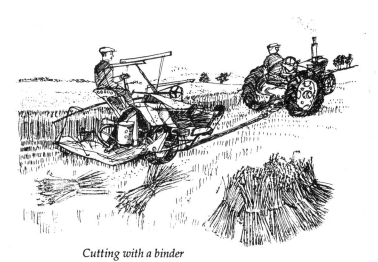

Cutting with a binder

7

'Now, boy,' said Charlie. 'Do you see that binder drop the shooves tied up with twine like this. Sometimes that don't properly, so you have to retie a shoove up. Holler like buggery if that start doing that. Pick up two shooves like this, one by one, ding their butts into the ground to make them hold a bit, push their heads together so they stick, and then they'll stand up. Then once you've got two a-standin', you can lean the rest against 'em.'

When he did it, that looked so easy. The sheaves seemed to stand by theirselves; they seemed to want to stand up. I tried it. I picked two sheaves up.

'Not by the binder twine!' shouted Charlie. 'You'll cut your hands like that and half the sods'll come undone.'

So I had to pick up the sheaves by grabbing the straw stalks; the stiff barley straw scraped my hands. Then I tried to strike the butts into the earth. The sheaves twisted about my hands as if they were alive: I couldn't get them to sit as I wanted them. Charlie chuckled. I pushed the stiff heavy heads together and they fell down, a mess. I tried again, three times, and at last I got two to stand up. But when I turned round to get two more, these first two slowly sank to the ground. Charlie danced, laughin', and I got angry with him.

'You'll get a hold on it in time,' he said, a bit more kindly, when he saw I was all red and sweaty with trying. 'Heh! Blast, he's fair melted with that!'

Then he and old Abbs started on the first row of stooks. I'd never seen anything like it. Old Charlie Bacon just swung his little old body along the row of sheaves. He wore an old flannel khaki shirt and washed-out corduroy trousers tied beneath the knee with string. His old boots were a sight, all coming apart at the seams and uppers. But couldn't he put them old sheaves in order! They stood up, as if he'd just ordered a row of soldiers to attention, and in no time there were six or eight stooks with ten or twelve sheaves in each, standing to dry in the sun, in a good row, leaving the stubble clean, and tidy. That old man! He went so fast! He had a wiry rhythm, a swing all of his own. He was like a little old gnome in one of them fairy stories that do a year's work in one afternoon.

So, I started a row of my own when the binder came round next. I closed my eyes against the dust and sweat, and I dug my hands into them hairy old sheaves, grasping them by their straw stalks in the body. I dinged them into the ground, and I found that if I drove them into the earth just as I shoved the heads together, they made a triangle and stayed up. Only sometimes even so they'd slide down, rustling and even coming undone. After an hour that suddenly came right to me. I could do it! So behind me were eight stooks, that stayed up, some of them looking a bit of a huddle, but never mind.

'Why, blast, boy,' said Charlie. 'Your stooks look as if the bloody old rats have bin at 'em.'

'Ho ... hum ... he've got the knackeroo of it, though,' gasped old Abbs. 'He've done a tidy bit already! Humph!'

So there they were, my sheaves, a bit wobbly, lined up beside the three rows he and old Abbs had done. How fast they moved around the field! How I admired them, Charlie and Abbo, as Charlie called him. Old Abbo was sweating, his big cheeks glistening, and his grey shirt all big round patches of dark wet. We couldn't decide whether to keep our shirts on or not. It was because it was barley, which was bristly with these brittle little whiskers that broke off. Charlie Bacon reckoned these barley awns were worse if you took your shirt off. Old Abbs thought that never made a difference, but Charlie wouldn't have that.

'Blast, boy,' he said, 'them old barley arns bite into you, whatever you do. They don't half rub you up. But if you go round with no top on, blast you'd be covered with 'em all over like a bloody hedgehog. A shirt do at least keep most of 'em off, but by Christ they get down yore neck, boy, don't they?'

'Blast,' said old Abbs, 'I'm all of a muckwash. They stick in your sweat like pishmares in the jam! They get in the small of your back and up your arse, and everywhere!'

Old Abbs' eyebrows were full of barley bits and they stuck to his sweat like extra beard bristles. Lord, they made him cough and gargle, too! If you look closely at these barley whiskers you can see they're more like a blade, a brittle little blade with hooks all along it. These snap off and break up, and these here little blades get into your shoes and socks, in all your sweaty creases, in your hair, and torment you. Every time you bang two sheaves together some of these awns fly off because you push your head into the top sheaf. But you work on and the prickly scratching becomes a pain you just live with, right down to your crutch and between your buttocks, and behind your knees. 'Tha's pukkaterry!' That's what Abbo said. And, yet, with the swing of it, and with the way you breathe deeper and deeper as you go, you get light-headed even despite the dust, and the harvest mites

9

biting you in between the scratches. That's funny how you can go on, though, when your eyes and nose are full of sweat, and them flies torment you. Every now and then, as we got round the field to a shady corner by the hedge, we'd stop for a bit and have a talk. At one stop the same two women came riding back up the road in the hot sun.

'How're you a-goin' on?' cried old Charlie. 'Do you want to come up and do a bit o' gleanin'?'

'Blast,' he said, when they had ridden away laughing, 'I'd like to chase them into them nettles. They wouldn't half heave about!'

'Why you old goot!' said Abbo. 'Hum! ... Ha! Ha!' He went off paralytic. I didn't think that was all that funny, but old Charlie he put on a silly face like he was some kind of prize tom cat.

At midday we had dinner under a big tree. Old Abbs passed round a yellow-glazed stone bottle of old ale that old Mrs had sent up with big pieces of bread and cheese, and ham. My skin was scrubbed and crusted with cold dried sweat now, and I felt like sharp ashes all over. But I was getting into the swing of it now and I was beginning to enjoy it. Old Charlie was even looking back over the lines of sheaves, as he turned up the big bottle and munched his bites.

'You can see the difference between his stooks and ours, Abbo, boy.'

'Ah, but he han't done so bad,' said old Abbs. 'Most o' his have stayed up any old how. Well done, boy!'

I loved old Abbs for that. I felt all warm and good in my inside. Donald the tractor driver had joined us now. Old Charlie ate a whole raw onion, nibbling bits off the end of his knife. He gave me a bit and it was a strong one: what with the onion and the dark beer and the strong cheese and the heavy sea air I felt I should burst, and I was beginning to feel healthy again. That old beer had a strong nutty flavour, and that squidged and bubbled in your mouth when you sucked it out of the bottle. Old Bacon and old Abbs stretched themselves out on their backs under the big shady sycamore and fell asleep straight away, and so did I. They had quite a job waking me at half past one, to get on with the harvesting. But I didn't feel any bad effects from the beer, 'cause you sweat that out of your system, old Abbs say. We all had what Abbo called a Jimmy Riddle before we set off.

The field stooked – we all fell asleep

The binder was going round and round, still in its cloud of dust, and the uncut island of barley grew smaller, and smaller. They had worked it out more or less when the field would be finished. Charlie thought they might finish at about five o'clock. So the word went round and up to the village, when the boy who brought the beer had gone back. At four o'clock people began to come up to the harvest field. There was old Abbs' wife, a plump woman in a blue dress with a black-speckled apron, and her younger sister. Then there were half a dozen boys, mostly in grey serge trousers or corduroy, some with caps. Isaac Walker the farmer came down with his twelve-bore shotgun, to see the end of the cutting. Old Charlie Bacon told me every one would get somethin' when they killed the rabbits and game in the field. As the binder went round, the rabbits, birds, hares and rats went further into the island of thick-standing barley to hide. Every now and then one o' these in a tizzy would make a bolt from the crop, running across the stubble towards the hedge. Then the tractor driver would stop the binder and jump off, and everyone would shout and holler to make the animal's fright worse, and confuse the creature so we could catch it. Sometimes that would try to hide in our stooks, and then we'd throw the sheaves down, to make 'em run out.

11

A rabbit ran into one of my stooks and I pulled the sheaves away. This here little old brown thing, mad with fear, ran straight towards Charlie, who fell on it. The rabbit squealed loudly, and my inside went all cold with fright, but old Charlie picked that up by the hind legs, so that it hung squealing and kicking from his hard old hand. Then, with his other hand spread out, he chopped the edge down hard on the back of the rabbit's neck and at once that was dead, and hung still.

'Ah,' said Charlie, looking appreciatively at the carcass with its white scut. 'He'll make a good meal an' all. Get a lot of them old milky does this time o' year: they're no bloody good. This here buck, he's all right.'

At first I was a bit sick about that poor rabbit, wonderin' what that was feelin': but then, all sweaty, in that hot sun, I just let myself go. The cutting went on faster now, the binder chattering and chattering, the stalks of corn being shuffled along the platform and being bundled up into sheaves and tied, and dropped off. Behind the binder the air was thick with corn dust and paraffin. We trudged round and round, setting up, and as the island of uncut corn shrunk there was this risin' excitement. How many rabbits would there be left in there?

Some of the boys had brought dogs: 'Keep that old dog on a lead,' shouted the tractor driver, 'or that binder'll cut his bloody legs off.'

But a rabbit did run into the blades, and screamed and screamed as it was caught by the machinery. Swearin', the driver got down with his stick and walloped it, breaking its skull so that it stopped squealing, and then poked what was left of it out of the metal spikes, and cutters.

'That one's turned into mincemeat, blast, Donald,' said Charlie.

'You could still make a bit o' stew out on it,' said old Abbs.

'Yew soft old bugger,' said Donald.

'Here, boy,' said Charlie, as the binder moved on in a cloud of dust, and one boy's black labrador growled as he ate the chopped up pieces of rabbit, skin and all. The stubble was all bloody and the rabbit Charlie had killed now swung lifelessly on a hook on the side of a box on the binder, where they kept the reels of twine.

Instead of feeling sick about the slaughter, I just got excited and wanted to catch more things to kill them. Up to now I had a

12

special feeling about the living things in the grass and the hedge-rows, and I had felt a kind of brother to them. I used to like just sitting down there in the grass waiting and watching for the wild things, and letting them be. But now I had joined in with the hunters, looking for something to kill and eat everywhere, so I was on the other side, so to speak. I found my heart was going fast and loud, and I wanted prey.

The boys all had big sticks and so I went over to the hedge and found myself a big dead piece of sapling, and kept that by me as I set up. Farmer Walker stood at one corner, where he could shoot away from the crop towards the wood: many of the animals would run that way and he'd be able to shoot clear of any people.

Suddenly a hare ran out. Two boys let their dogs go. The hare zigzagged and then tore straight off towards the wood, throwing up dust from the stubble. Mr Walker couldn't shoot and the hare easily outstripped the dogs. I was glad. Them silly old dogs fussed at the hedge and barked, but by this time the hare was half-way up through Glandford Woods. Perhaps everything would get away? I half hoped they would. I reckoned the animals were all frightened badly in there in that last shrinking stand of barley.

Most of them weren't going to get away. Two rats made a bolt for it, and the sticks were out. One rat nearly made it, running away from a boy: but he got in a glancing blow and tipped it over showing the pale under-belly. At once, two boys beat it to death. A rabbit came right out in front of me, like a rush of brown smoke. I kicked at it and caught it off balance. That swerved and seemed to escape me; but then, in its panic, it stopped. I heard myself hollering, as if it were someone else, and saw two boys running towards me to get it. They weren't going to have my rabbit. I rushed across the stubble, stumbling and fell on it. I could feel that struggling against my hot shirt and it gave a stifled squeal.

'Come here you!' I shouted, as if he were someone human. That took quite a struggle to get hold of its hind legs and it scratched me so that the blood ran. I was angry then. I stood up and my eyes went all red, the whole landscape seemed dark. For some time that rabbit curled up in leaps, struggling, and wouldn't hang down straight so I could rabbit-punch its neck. Suddenly that seemed to give up, and I brought my hand down sharply like Charlie on the back of its head. For a few seconds it quivered and jumped like some electric thing, and then hung still. But then I felt cold and wretched;

but pleased, too, because everyone had seen me kill that rabbit.

'Blast, you've a-done it, boy!' said old Charlie Bacon laughing. 'Whoops! Ho! Ho! Ho! Tha's a good one an' all. He have got th' idea, townee tho' he is!'

He felt the chest of my rabbit with his sinewy old hands. And he was off after another brown furry little old thing, running among the legs of the people. Some of the boys got so excited they just stood there and the rabbits even ran between their legs.

At last the binder had only one long thin rectangle of barley to do, and the creatures came out one after the other. There was a pheasant in there, that got its legs cut off, and Mr Walker had to shoot that as it flopped about crying. There were three more hares, a dozen rats and twenty rabbits. Two of the hares got away, and one rabbit, chased by a dog to the hedge; fortunately it didn't swerve, or stop to think. That shot through the hedge like a cannon ball, with a puff of dust. I was just behind it, and threw myself into the bottom of the hedge after it – and as the dust cleared I saw something gleam inside one of the holes: I couldn't say what it was, but I could only say to myself there's something sticking out down that hole, some metal thing, that's a rum un. I didn't think about it at the time, because my eyes were full of sweat and I really had my blood up. I killed one more rabbit with my stick. I hit that so hard I broke the stick and broke the rabbit's back.

Now we laid them all out in rows on the stubble to be shared. Charlie was given the pheasant, and old Abbs a hare and a rabbit. Mr Walker took a hare and a rabbit, and that left everyone else a rabbit each, more or less, whether they'd caught one or not. The binder driver had a hare, and then he joined us to help finish stookin'. He give someone else my rabbit but I switched that over when no one was lookin', so I took my rabbit home to Mrs Isaac. By six o'clock that was all done. My hands and arms were all splashed with blood and my shirt was all wet with sweat. Inside it there was a thick crust of barley blades. I felt my old Mum wouldn't recognise me as I walked up the lane with my rabbit swinging in my hand. I was a real country lad now.

14

TWO

That first day on Isaac Walker's farm brought out one side of my character. I'm a Norfolk boy and I live in Norwich, and go to the City of Norwich School. My father work in Norwich for a firm that make bicycles, only his family come from Melton Constable, where his father used to make railway wagons, so he and his brothers grew up in the countryside. My grandfather's brother, Tom, is a real country-man – he's a steward on Sir Alfred Jodrell's estate at Bayfield Hall, and he can tell by looking at a tree how many cubic feet of timber there is in it. It was through Uncle Tom that I got fixed up to go and stay at Isaac Walker's farm at Letheringsett just down the road from Glandford where Tom lived, and I'll be telling you a lot more about him and his wife, old Anna.

I got into bad odour with Uncle Tom and that was a terrible thing, as you'll find out.

But I was in trouble, anyway, this year: it's 1938 and the new City Hall in Norwich has just been opened by His Majesty the King. We all had to go and sit there to see him do it, all the school stretched out along wooden benches along the front of the hall, where there was some big bronze lions. They were the cause of the trouble. The girl's High School were behind us, and the backsides of these lions stuck out towards us, and you could see all their rude parts, so we couldn't help ourselves from making remarks about this, and I got really silly about it. My history master told me off, and I kept on joking and messing about, so he and I fell out terribly after this disgraceful event.

'Virtually under the eye of a visiting sovereign,' he kept saying. 'You disgraced your school, Roland Ransome.'

I liked history before this, but now I went right off it. I got bad marks in the mock Certificate and then I got ill: I got 'flu and bronchitis, and I got so low my old Mum and Dad thought they'd send me to recuperate on a farm. They put it to Uncle Tom one day, when we were over at Glandford on a visit to him and Anna.

'That's funny you should say that,' Uncle Tom said, 'I was talking to old Isaac Walker in the Bell last night and he was sayin'

15

how his eldest boy had gone away to start his own small-holdin'. He say, "There's that empty room, and my old woman, she've got nothin' to do except feed me and the chickens. I shall have to do bed-and-breakfasts," he said.'

'I don't think the farmers have done too well this year,' said my Aunt Anna. 'They're glad of any penny they can get. If you was to pay him a little bit, he'd be glad to have the boy for a while, I dare say.'

'He could help him cut the corn for him,' said Tom. 'Can you use a scythe, boy?'

This was a great joke, though I couldn't see the point yet – that is, till I tried to use one on the farm, and nearly cut my leg off first time I swung it and tripped over.

'We'll go and ask old Isaac after dinner.'

'He is a good old farmer,' said Anna. 'Good as gold – only he's a little bit near …' she added, after reflection. 'He treat his men alright, only he can't afford to give them much of a largers. And he keep most of the game for hisself, of course.'

Anyway, Isaac Walker agreed that afternoon to have me on his farm for three weeks, bed and board, for thirty shillings a week. That seemed a lot of money those days and I was a-going to work in the harvest field. Once that was settled my old Uncle Tom and my old Dad and old Isaac Walker, they kept pinchin' my arm muscles and laughing, with all that kind of squit.

'You'll have your corn done twice as quick, Isaac, this year, blast!'

'Har!' said the farmer, showing his green old teeth. He looked all scrawny in his neck and hands, I thought, but he had a decent old face. I looked at his face hard and he didn't seem to have nothing nasty in him, though he didn't say over much, so he didn't give himself away.

The next weekend my Dad was to take me over on Sunday night in his old car. My old Dad, he was one of the first in our family to have a car – that was a 'Hands' tourer with a cloth hood you could push back and celluloid side windows. That had a handle in the front to start it up. Every now and then we'd take a run out to Glandford village. There was this little old flint and brick house called the Readin' Room that my uncle looked after for the village, as well as doin' his work on the Estate. Their cottage was joined on to that, and sometimes we used to drive out for Sunday dinner. My old Dad like testing his car up Edgefield Hill – that's about the only hill in Norfolk, I think.

I used to love those trips. My old Mum said you could smell the sea when you got near Cley: you'd catch the air of the salt marshes up there. You knew you were getting near the sea because the light gets so bright, and the sun on any house that's white-washed, that nearly blind you. Anyhow, I was always mortal hungry by the time we got near Aunt Anna's, Sunday dinner time. As soon as we got out with our noses all stretched out, there'd be this marvellous smell comin' out of her kitchen.

My old Mum, she'd always arrive with a basket full of stuff: she'd bring old Anna foreign fruit off Norwich market, oranges and bananas, and some marmalade or mince pies she'd made. Then my old Dad would bring Uncle Tom a battery lamp or an accumulator for his wireless set, or something like that, and then we'd all shamble in through the gate and past the well, with old Anna kissing my Mum and me, and sayin' 'Hullo, my little man! Why how he do grow, Tom! Bless my heart alive!' Then she'd push and pull me about like anything.

I could put up with all this, on account of the smell of that dinner she was cooking. We turned down the path to her kitchen door, and there the full force of her cookery would hit you. She had a high brick oven in the wall behind a door painted black with a brass knob, and in this she'd be cooking bread and cakes. Then there was a metal range all polished with Zebo graphite and shining like a gun. This would have a bright coal fire going in the grate, and out of this range came the smell of roast beef or roast rabbit or pig's fry, together with roast potatoes and Yorkshire pudding, apple pie, or baked custard. When the scent of all these vittals hit you all at once, you would have nearly died droolin' over them.

Her cooking was so rich because my Aunt would use every-thing of the best: yeast and butter, strong flour and dripping, local farm meat, fresh eggs and vegetables straight out of Tom's neat little old garden plot up the back, and the hen shed we always got shown around. Tom would stroke his whiskers and take us round his rows of peas and beans, vegetables that always looked as if they were being grown for a show, the onions were so fat, and the pea pods so plump and shiny green. He had them black and white speckled hens, North Holland Blues, and one or two little old bantams what shruck murder all day when they crowed.

17

Anna would look uneasy and say, 'I did pig's fry today. I don't know if young Duffy like pig's fry, that en't everybody's taste is that?' and there I would be fainting to get at the liver and sweetbready bits of it, even the crinkly bit of skirty fat, as soon as we could be sat down and served. We ate in a little drawing room where Tom had a big oval mahogany table, and they laid out their best silver on a pure white tablecloth. Anna'd have her bread out by now, coolin' on a rack, and the smell of that there was enough to drive you half-rocked with hunger.

On the walls were photographs of people in the family: Tom with the altar he had built in the village church; my Grandad William with a railway wagon he'd built; one or two cousins or brothers with their babies all wrapped up like puddings. Then there was a sailing ship done in coloured wool at sea; and some grey pictures of women stepping across stones with mountains in the background, and some big old shaggy stags on a moor. Uncle Tom had a couple of silver candlesticks: real silver they were, all twisted round in knots. And all the furniture was of the best mahogany 'cause my old Uncle Tom was a cabinet maker, and knew when a thing was properly made.

'Yes,' said my old Mum, coming to the surface as soon as she'd got herself round a piece of pig's liver. 'He is a-growin' fast.'

'No doubt,' said Anna, 'he have outgrown his strength, poor boy. Do you have some more of these here little parsnips,' she added, 'my little man. They've only just come out of the garding.'

Anna seemed to think I could be fattened up straight away, so that when I went out after dinner my legs wouldn't be thin and stalky any longer. However, I never minded, and I used to have three or four helpings.

It was after one of these Sunday dinners we fixed up for me to stay with old Isaac Walker.

THREE

'We thought that would do the boy to come out and work on a farm during harvest time. So we thought we'd ask you for some ideas off of you and Anna, Tom.'

Uncle Tom wiped his mouth and moustache carefully with his big white handkerchief, and turned to look my mother closely in the face.

My old Uncle Tom was a big man who used always to wear a black or dark grey worsted suit with a waistcoat and those kind of stripey flannel shirts you fastened a collar to. His wife Anna was much smaller than he was, like a little old nippy. She had been a dairy maid, and she knew how to make butter. She had a big wooden churn with a handle to turn that round in her scullery. She knew everything about cooking and baking. She had a bright, happy face and cheeks like English apples, always bright and shiny, rosy with effort and the sun. Her eyes were bright and eager, and she had that kind of face that's always looking forward to something. She didn't just take in the things round her, and look worried about them, which is how my old Mum always looked. Aunt Anna's bright little old eyes always seemed to be looking out of the windows expecting something really lovely to be coming down the street. But then she was always making excuses for not being better prepared for you, saying this wasn't ready, and that wasn't ready, and she didn't know whether there'd be enough, and why didn't Tom take our coats off us and the kitchen was a poor place for everyone to sit in, and so on: only while she went on like this we were as happy as anything just to be there.

Tom wore big black boots and a heavy silver watch chain. I'm getting too old for that sort of thing now, of course, but when I was little he used to take out this big watch on the end of that chain and press a button and that used to make that chime just like a church clock. And on the bit of his chain he had big fobs, seals and that, cut bits of red and blue stone with twisted gold settings. He'd let me look at all this and the watch, and hold it, but not for long, because that had to be back into his waistcoat pocket to look right. He had a big ruddy face with a moustache, and he used to wax the ends and draw them up in sharp points. His cheeks were red and covered with little blue vein lines. He had a heavy blue beard stubble, but his hair had gone rather thin on top: he wore a cap out of doors and this pressed down the few lines of hair on his head. He didn't like taking his cap off, because he was a bit bald: there's a photograph of him still hanging in the Shell Museum in Glandford showing him when Queen Mary came down to open it in 1935 when it was her Jubilee. My old Uncle Tom didn't even take his cap off for her.

Though I called him Uncle Tom, he was really my Great Uncle. At Bayfield Hall he not only looked after all the timber, but also the game and the trout in the River Glaven. To my old Dad, Uncle Tom stood for everything he would have liked to have been, because he would much rather have lived in the country than in Norwich.

My poor old Dad! I could see that when we were fixing it up he looked as though he'd rather have been in my place. He hadn't made any plans for his holiday, except to muck about in the garden, see City football team play, go fishing at Coltishall and drive over to see his brother in Birmingham. He was glad at any rate he would be able to do most of these without me, because I could never see anything on the terraces at the Nest, so I used to grumble all the way through the match, waiting to go home. As for fishing I got so bored I used to throw stones in the river and scare all the fish for miles away. He hated fishing when he had to take me.

Any old how, my name's Roland Ransome and I live at Mile Cross, near Norwich, and I'm an old boy now because I'm coming up to fifteen.

I don't like my real name – Roland: that's too fancy. My old Mum was reading some romantic book when I was on the way, she told me. Anyway, she stuck to that but no old boy can go around with a soft name like Roland so they call me Roly, or sometimes Duff, because of Roly-Poly and a duff is a puddin', do you see? I don't know that I don't like it any better being called Duffy, because some of 'em when they're in a nasty mood make that into Duffer. Old Do-do (Mr Doe, our form master at school) he sometimes called me Duff, and then he say Duffer, Duffest, and he think that's ever so funny, only I don't. I don't mind Duffy, though, at least when that name is used in a kind sort of way and, any road, at least I aren't called a Norfolk dumplin' or swimmer.

20

And now I have to come to the other side of my character. All right, I can be a country boy, even if they do take it out of me at times. But, although I fell out with my history master over the lions' testicles, I'm also a reader, and I'm very interested in History and in Natural History.

I like watching things and thinking about things. It's because of that, I reckon, I got landed with the name Duffy: people see me sitting and thinking, and they think I'm dim or stupid. But there are days when I lie on my back looking up at the clouds for hours on end, and I aren't just blank or dreaming: I'm thinking about time and the world or about death, and things like that – I don't tell anyone about this. I couldn't talk about it to anyone. But I do. So, when they set about me, and go for me as if I were lazy or stupid, I just think to myself how they just don't know how busy my head is, inside.

The masters at school go on: Roly do that, Duffy have you finished that page of sums, Duffy stay behind and see me, but I've been in a different world altogether, and a lot of things happen in that grass country that don't belong to the ordinary life of daytime at all. When I come home my old Mum say, 'What have you been doin', Roly?' and I say 'Nothin.' But when I get in the bath and lie there with all the nettle stings smarting beautiful and the blood soaking off the briar scratches, looking over my blue bruises on my legs, I think about all the adventures I've had, and she don't know nothing about it, and never will.

A lot of the things you can't tell old people, not like your old Mum nor the schoolmasters. Sometimes I spend ever such a long time just looking at one thing. That's all new to me – but, of course, they'd think you're a sawney. Take watching a spider. The other day I sat out the back by our hedge all one afternoon. I was watching one of them stripey garden spiders. She had put out lines to four or five points on the fence, just like someone beginning to put up a circus tent. Then she went round and round, starting in the middle, and she made these little rectangles, stopping at each place where the ropes crossed, as if she was doing a knot. She walked down to the ground and up a long stalk, and made a connection up there: how did she know that if she went up there she'd be able to get the right angle on her engineering construction? What kind of mind does a spider have? I couldn't do it, I know that. Then when she'd finished she went off in a corner and waited, just like my old Dad do when he throws his hook and line out, and watch the float for that to go bob,

21

bob, what tell him he's got a bite.

Well, after a while along come a fly and that go head over heels into the net, and make a hole in it. But that old fly is caught by the leg, and after a bit of buzzin' she stop to have a think. Then she rush out, all her stripey football socks going, she laid hold on him with her spikey feet. This is the bit I like: she smell him and then she bite him. Then she wait a bit till that take effect like when the dentist jab you in your gum. Then she spin him round and round and wind him up, with her spikey toes, so he's just like a leaf in tissue paper. That's a masterpiece. But think how long that would take, to tell that to your old Mum. So when she ask me what I been doin' after I've been watching something like that, I say 'Nothin''. How could I say to her I'd just been watchin' one little old spider all mornin'?

Then, of course, they think you're a lazy little devil, or stupid, or like they say in the school reports 'must work harder'. Anyway, there's a lot going on in my life that they never know about. Only sometimes that lead to difficulties.

I think too much I reckon – that's my trouble. While I can kill a rabbit with the rest of them, I don't like seeing things die. There's an old rabbit running round the lawn now, just as I'm writing this, and he keep stopping and sitting up, he've got something nasty on his toes, and he keep licking 'em and biting 'em, to get that off. Then he shake his front leg, flip, flop, to get that off, fleas perhaps. Only the way he shakes himself, that remind me of how, when they die, they kick and kick and shudder and judder, and that make me feel humble, and I know I'll think about that at night when I'm alone in the dark. So, when I'm out in the fields, as you'll see, I go after 'em and clout 'em on the head with a stick, just like anyone else, and then when they're cooked, I'll eat the lot, heart and brains and all, in a stew or roast with a bit o' thyme stuck inside 'em, I am in two minds. My old Mum say I'm a mass of contradixions, which is much the same as what my old Dad say, only he say I'm an awkward little bugger – and that's a word, by the way, you mustn't mind here because they always use it in Norfolk.

He was ever so quiet as we drove over to Letheringsett, except to tell me to mind my manners and not to get my feet wet. My old Dad carried in the suitcase with my clothes in it and handed over my rubber boots to Mrs Walker. Then he said he'd call back for me in three weeks' time. I could see he felt funny, because his face was a bit drawn – I'd never been away from home before and I could see he was going to miss me. I felt a bit watery at the knees and all, after he'd gone, but that didn't last long, because I was that excited.

The farm was called Home Farm. The house and barns were built of flint and brick – flints mostly, big cobbles carted off the beaches, I reckon, and stuck together with cement. And there were walls everywhere – I've never seen so many walls. The farmhouse was in the middle of the village, which is just two miles from Holt. The other houses in the village were also built of flint and brick. And then a wall started that ran pretty well all the way to Glandford, past the whole length of Bayfield Hall, all round the estate. What that must have cost, up hill and down dale like that! There was an entrance by the farm and from my bedroom I could see the drive road to the Hall run down into a wood, then by the end of a big lake. Up above the lake there's a huge red brick house about two hundred years old: that's Bayfield Hall, and at the south end of that there's a ruined chapel. You can see the little bell cage, that's all overgrown with ivy, and so are all the walls, all broken down and crumbled. My Great Granny Bayfield she lived up above there, deep in the woods, Uncle Tom's mother.

Home Farm was about a mile from the Hall and stood just where the wall runs into Letheringsett village. The roof was made of thick, dark blue shiny tiles and the walls of cobbles with red brick courses. At the back are big yards and barns, and the whole outfit look solidly built and well looked after, with everything handsome about it. All the barns and the walls were built with red brick borders and big stretches of black and white flint, and the house itself surrounded by great big trees. They didn't have no bathroom. I had to wash in cold water in that china basin in my bedroom. But I did wash, to show I'd been brought up properly and to get the grumbles out of my eyes.

FOUR

We had supper in the kitchen, boiled bacon and boiled potatoes with big cups of strong reddish-brown tea and bread and butter, and a piece of cheese after. The kitchen was painted pea green with yellow curtains. They just cleared a space for meals among the boxes of cartridges, samples of feed, corn in paper bags, keys and secateurs, tools for ringing animals' noses and punching holes in their ears, powders for killing fleas, baskets for collecting eggs, crayons and pencils, and piles of circulars and notebooks. How old Isaac ever sorted out his accounts at the end of the year I couldn't think, or how he found anything. There must have been some system about it, though, because anytime he wanted to put his hand on anything, he could.

Anyway, Mrs Walker was all over me about that rabbit I brought home. She started as soon as I stepped outside in the yard to wash my hands and tried to shake some of the barley horns out of my hair, and get the sweaty old stuff out of my neck.

'What a clever little man,' she said, her face all crumpled up with smiles. 'Catchin' a rabbit in the piece like that, why he must have gone a lamperin' over them quicks like nobody's business. I shan't stint for wittles while he's here, that I on't. I on't be needin' to eke out with swimmers like Mrs Liddamore, allus fillin' her men up wi' tarnips or plump or dumplin's, or old muck like that room o' good quality meat, mind you I got nawthin' against dumplin's when tha's parky weather. Tha's a good fat little old buck rabbit – we'll have him Friday and you kin have a nice bit o' hinderpart Duffy boy.'

'Ah,' I said, because I never understood a word of hers hardly, and was too tired hardly to eat my supper let alone listen to her talk. So when we'd done they said I could go to bed and I was glad. Mr and Mrs Walker came up to bed as soon as that got dark, which was about half-past nine. That saved paraffin in the lamps. I went to bed with a candle.

I had a good look around my bedroom for the first time. The floor was just boards except for a little old rug from Bonds in

Norwich and there was the bed, a chair, and one big cupboard in the wall by the chimney. There was a little black grate and there were some white curtains on wooden curtain rings, and on the other side of the fireplace the washstand with a china bowl in it. Over the fireplace was a big mirror all spotty with damp and fly muck. It was in this bedroom I felt the strangest: that was the only place where I felt homesick, because that wasn't like my bedroom at home. At home I had all my books and my things, like a steam motor boat that wouldn't go any more, but I liked to think about the times when it did go, with its smell of meths and hot oil. And there were some things tucked out of sight that I didn't tell anyone much about, like my teddy bear who was all worn smooth and was greasy black in places on his nose and belly, but no one threw him away.

I didn't have any of them things at the farm because I didn't bring them, and I didn't have nothing that reminded me of home, except the smell of myself in bed. Once I got into bed and smelt myself under the clothes, I felt at home again, in the dark, and stopped feeling homesick.

Home Farm

25

FIVE

Next day we had to get all the sheaves lifted out of the stooks and put into a stack. After that, when all the stacks were up we'd take a threshing machine up there to separate the barley grains out of each stack and leave the straw. Every sheaf had to be handled four times – up from behind the binder into the stook, from the stook on to the cart, from the cart to the stack, and then from the stack into the threshing machine. There was plenty of work on the farms at that time of year, as you can see, and that all depended on good weather to do it in. It was no good stacking or threshing wet corn. We didn't get to work on the field till midday when the dew had dried off a bit so we could start stackin' the shooves.

All this was done with a pitchfork, a long pole with two sharp prongs on the end, about a hand's breadth apart. They were polished and shone, and the long handle was made of ash. A sheaf of barley was about three foot long and weighed about a stone. That was thick and stalky at the butt end, and shaggy at the top or grain end. You had to be able to pick up a sheaf so that it balanced on the end of your pitchfork. You should then be able to swing it up so that that fell on the cartload more or less in place: someone stood in the cart to pack the sheaves, butts outwards, all round the cart. As you built the load, the thicker butt ends had to be round the edges of the cart, because they were bulkier than the heads, so that the loads sloped inwards to the centre. This should make it stable, as the cart lumbered over the rough stubble ground. The load would sway from side to side anyway, but if the butts were outwards the load would tend to slip to the middle. If the load was built badly it would topple over and all the sheaves would have to be picked up again. And every time the sheaves fell about, some grain would be lost, knocked out of the head – that would be 'shed'.

Then, when the load of corn reached the stack, all the sheaves had to be lifted and placed again, in the same way. As the stack got higher, we'd use an elevator, with a little put-put motor, to take the sheaves up a blue thing, like a mechanical ladder, to the top. The corn

26

had to be just right for the stack – not too wet or it would heat up. The farm workers would test a stack by thrusting an iron bar through it. If the stack had overheated, the iron got too hot to hold. If it was too hot when it was pulled out, the whole stack would have to be quickly dismantled and, if the worst happened, all the straw would be going mouldy and bad, even black, and of course the grain in the head would be spoiled.

There was a lot to mind about when you used a pitchfork. You had to be careful you didn't stick that in anyone's face or into his thigh or into your foot, or other people's feet. If you used that clumsily, you could break up a sheaf and the straw would go everywhere. Old Charlie Bacon could kill rats with his, spearing them like cheese on a toasting fork. It gave you a good feeling when you got a sheaf balanced right on your fork and you had the swing of it. The heavy bundle of barley seemed to fly up in the air and land exactly where you wanted it. But if you tried to lift a sheaf that was lying under another sheaf, or if you tried to lift the one you were standing on, Lord, that would give you gyp: you could really hurt your insides heaving at the tightly packed straw when nothing would move.

'Ogh!' I'd say.

'Well, blast,' old Abbs would say. 'Humph ... Do you're tryin' to lift the bloody shoove you're a-standin' on, what the hell do you expect, boy?'

'He rightly expect to goo flyin' into th' air!' old Bacon would say, 'like one o' them old dirigibles.'

'Allus pick the one on top,' said old Abbs kindly. 'Otherwise, boy, you'll pull yor bloody old guts out by th' end of the day.'

But I still did it, every now and then, and that made me desperate. Then I'd just try to get one up and my strength would give out. If you got a sheaf flying up, well balanced, that would tuck into place. If you heaved at one that was caught, that sheave would be sluggish and that would seem sluggish all the way up, so that seemed that weighed half a ton. Then perhaps your strength would give out, and the sheaf would go sailin' down on the ground, thump!

'Gawd, boy!' old Charlie would shout. 'You'll knock all the bloody barley out of it – old Isaac he'll come along and fair crack his jaw at us. Lord, bless my heart alive, if he sees all that grain shed, he'll take that outer our wages!'

It had been such a blue day, that I was surprised to see tall

27

towers of cloud, rising about the wood to the west as the sun declined.

'Hallo, hallo,' said Charlie. 'Do you know, boy, we're a-goin' to have a bloody old tempest?'

The cloud turrets were enormous. I could see that. They must have been twenty miles away, but their tops curled over towards us, high into the sky. That was a good job we had finished the field: the barley heads were heavy and would have been laid by heavy rain, so that they would have gone mouldy or started to sprout in the ear. But after all that work, it didn't look as if we were going to have a quiet night to sleep it off.

The storm didn't come as quickly as I had expected. Those tall towers of cloud must have been further away than I thought. They must have been really right up to the moon. We hadn't seen anything but blue sky for weeks and weeks. But that harvest day had been a scorcher, the kind of day when the sun really burns you.

I was just dropping off that night when it began. There was this distant noise of rumbles and bangs, as if some big iron water tanks were being rolled down a cliff. I tried to go to sleep in spite of it, because I was very tired, and maybe I did go off for a while, because nothing seemed to happen. Maybe, I thought, that will go away: sometimes in Norfolk storms went straight out to sea and missed the land altogether. Then I came back to the surface and heard a long snarly sort of growl that echoed off the wood. It looked as if we were going to get that after all. I thought I ought to say my prayers. I hadn't said my prayers for a long time. I wasn't sure if there was much point in saying them. I had prayed for two 'goods' in my end of term tests at school and all I got was two passes – one wasn't very good at all: so I'd put off praying for a bit until I'd thought that out. But then I got guilty because I thought that was trying to put pressure on the Almighty and I knew that was wrong. But then what was the point of praying if nothing was going to come of it? However, now I thought I might get struck by lightnin' before I'd puzzled out these problems, so that might be a good insurance to have a little pray. So I heaved myself up in bed on my knees under the blankets. I wasn't going to get out and kneel on the floor, not with a storm like that coming up. So I said a comfortable 'Our Father' and hoped that would do, and that the Lord wouldn't mind me being a bit lazy. My Granny always called Him 'the Lord' when she went to chapel.

After I'd done that it began to rain, just a steady hiss at first. But then there was a flash and after a while a long rumble of thunder, and the rain started coming down faster: I've noticed that before, that the rain changes pace after a lightning strike. So it began to make a heavy shushing noise, and then to drum, really thump hard on the windows. And at first there were some really bright flashes, and the thunder roared in the rain. I could smell I was sweating with fear now, and my mouth was going dry.

I hate storms. I have done ever since I was ever so little. My old Mum told me once that when I was two and my little brother Sam was born and we had a nurse in, and this nurse was looking after me, there was a bad storm, and this nurse went right out of her mind. She left something burning on the stove and that caught fire but she just lay about having hysterics. Then a bit later my poor brother Sam died. So, whenever there's a storm, I can't help it, I think the world is coming to an end, what with one thing and another. So, now the storm started, I got in the cupboard and pulled the door on to myself. I didn't know what there might be in there – I hadn't looked and I didn't dare. I could feel some coats and things round me, and the smell of old Mrs' mothballs nearly choked me. But I got right in there, and pulled the door to, to shut out the lightning best I could. Only I couldn't get it right close, and so when there was a flash I could see a long streak where the crack was in the door.

These flashes were blue now and pink, and the noise came very soon after the flash, so the storm was right over this part of Norfolk. I knew how to work that out from my Children's Encyclopaedia: seven seconds between the flash and the thunder was one mile. Now there come a wind, a howling wind that drove the water against the window panes in great churning thumps and roared in the trees outside. The noise was deafening: the thunder was continuous now, which I'd never heard and the wind tore and groaned in the trees, and the rain lashed and lashed at the windows.

Then the lightning became that sort that goes 'Frapp!' like a whiplash without any pause between the flash and the thunder. That just sounds like a steel sword being beaten on the trunk of a huge beech tree, only reachin' right up to heaven. There was one of these 'Frapp!' flashes about every fifteen seconds and the house was shaking with the continual thunder, and the wind: all the elements seemed to be trying to paste one another over the head. I was trembling and dripping with sweat, and I was praying inside my mind that, if I survived this storm, I'd be as good as God wanted me to be for ever more. I'd never done so much prayin' in my life, not countin' seconds. 'Oh God!' I was murmuring. 'Make that go away, one, two, three, four ...'

But after an hour or so the storm eased up, and there was a pause while the thunder rolled about round the sky, a bit less solid. But then that came back, with a solid drench of rain, and I thought the panes would never stand it this time. As it was, the rainwater was all seething and bubbling through the crack at the bottom of the sash window. We had a dozen or more of them cracky old flashes, like Almighty God was throwin' fire bolts at the farm but then, by degrees, that grew a bit more distant again. I kept looking at my luminous wrist-watch and thinking if I survive till five in the morning this will be the greatest miracle of my life. But in the end the storm went on till half-past three, and after that there was nothing but a few pink flickers, and a grumble or two. The trees were still full of water, you could hear: everything was dripping and dripping. At last I got back into bed and went to sleep as my sweat dried. But now I had to keep that bargain, to be good for ever. That made me thoughtful: how was I to know every time what it was to be good? I reckoned if I counted up to twenty every time and prayed a bit at the same time, I might make the right good choice. But as soon as the sun came out and all the moisture started to steam away, and I thought ah, well, these storms are only so much steam and air after all, I forgot all about that old rigmarole.

So, I was in a right funny old mood when I got up about six. That storm had been so dreadful that I had gone right over to my other character, the one who thought long and hard about things he'd seen and went round and round things while wondering about time and nature, and death. Suddenly, a memory came into my head: I had seen something gleam in that rabbit hole. What was it? As I told you, when I had been a-runnin' one of them rabbits down, I had seen something in one of the warrens. I reckoned I must go and see what that was, now everyone was gone home. Yesterday, with all the excitement and keepin' an eye on my rabbit, I hadn't been able to go back to the hole. This was the one good thing I recollected in the night, in the middle of the storm. I decided to go up to the field before breakfast, before anyone was about, and see what that was.

My heart! That was wet and soggy everywhere! But the sun was coming up and that was bright enough. There were swidges of water all along each side of the lane. I often used to get up early like this and go off with my nose to the ground. When I'm in that kind of mood I like chewing grass. I like pulling the stalk of a thick, long piece of grass out of its sort of sheath and chewing that when it's juicy; the pale end you can nearly see through like glass. My old Mum says that's dangerous, because of 'anthrax'. If animals get anthrax then they piddle on the grass and the anthrax get on the grass where animals have been piddling, so I make sure I get a nice clean stem to chew. If you bite that sideways, up the stem about six inches, you get a lot of juice out of a bent.

There are a lot of other things to look for in the country that you can do to get a taste of good stuff. For instance, in the spring there's bread and cheese. Cheese is the first long green shoots of brambles. You have to get a juicy bit and peel it with a sharp knife, taking all the thorns off. You eat the middle bit. The 'bread' is the little hawthorn leaf shoots, just before they open, the first green buds of the year in the hedge. You wait till they're opening, like little moths, then you pinch them off and eat them. That isn't much good after the middle of May, though, because they get big and tough.

In July there's a tall bluey green plant with a kind of shaggy, furry stuff at the top, which you can roll like tobacco and smoke. This feel just like tobacco when you crush it in your hand and rub it: that's called Mugwort. That all break up and feel just like the stuff your old Dad push in his pipe. That's horrible when you smoke it. You can get an old clay pipe – you find them in the earth in old cottage gardens or perhaps you'll find a pipe on the beach – I did, a good rosewood pipe, with a silver band. This herb taste like burnt straw when you light it, and that make your mouth all drawn up and smoky. But that feel as if you're a real smoker and that's all free. I had tins of the stuff, but that all went mouldy so I put that on the fire, and I just kept the sore throat.

Turnips are good, and sugarbeet. You have to wipe the dirt off and just chew into them. Some people gnaw into mangolds, but I won't go beyond swedes. You just chew the pulp and then spit that out: same with unripe apples. The best wild fruit is blackberries, of course, in September. You get to know where the fat ones are and there's pounds of them if you know where to look, and of course mushrooms only you want to make sure they're brown underneath otherwise you die – unless you eat twenty-four rabbit stomachs chopped up, so they say.

All the branches and bushes were full of water, that morning, so if you bumped against anything you got soaked: loads of water kept coming down out of the trees in the morning breeze. My shoes were black and wet, and the bottoms of my trousers were soaked before I got fifty yards, so I didn't care any more. After that, that didn't matter, though I walked in the road a lot, so as not to get any wetter. I looked over the hedge at our field and despite all the squalls in the storm, only two stooks had fallen over, one of mine, and one of Charlie's and old Abbs'. As my footsteps rang on the asphalt road that was steaming in the hot sun, I saw a rabbit run across the fields and shoot into that hole again. I laughed. I wondered if that was the same rabbit? I thought perhaps he was wondering what had happened to twenty of his friends?

When I got to the warren I could have a good look at it. That must have been an enormous underground network, stretchin' all along the bank. There were holes everywhere and I couldn't be sure that the heavy rain had washed some of the holes even wider, and now I saw the right hole: I remembered now that had a creeping plant with a purple flower above it, which I'd noticed yesterday even though I was so excited. And there was this gleaming bit I'd noticed at the back of the hole.

I got down on my knees to the hole and got hold of it. It was metal. At first I thought it might be something from the '14–18' war. After a jerk or two, I levered it out of the earth. It was a big twisted shape and crusted over, and earthy and brown, about nine inches long. But where the rabbits had been scrapin' they'd scraped the dirt off the long part, and what showed through was bright metal. I couldn't think what it might have been used for or why it should be down a rabbit warren on Isaac Walker's farm. That had a twirly kind of decoration in one place, like one of Uncle Tom's fobs, and the whole thing seemed to be twisted regular, round and round. I don't know how I knew it, but I knew it was gold, and was very old.

Now, the reason why my history master was so annoyed with me, fooling around at the Royal visit, was because the week before he'd taken us all to the British Museum. He had spent a lot of time organising this and he had met with a lot of resistance. That had meant quite an expense from parents, and three hours on the train: he had put over a lot of stuff about how it was a training in responsibility for these adolescents, and all that. So, he was fed up with me for going back to being childish again.

On the trip he'd told me about the Dark Ages, and how he thought they weren't all dark at all. There were these Anglo-Saxons and he reckoned they had reached a high level of life. We talked all the way in the train, me and old Cave. And in the museum the most beautiful things were torques, neck decorations from burial mounds in East Anglia. They were simple, curved pieces of bright gold, twisted in a fluted way to make them gleam, with curved ends, for women to put round their necks.

The object in Mr Walker's warren was exactly the same. That was an Anglo-Saxon torque, I reckoned. I felt all queer down my legs and in my stomach when I recognised it, and I looked round at the big sweeps of stubble field and the woods – and they seemed to have been smoothed and worn by a thousand years passing over them since this ornament was buried there.

I just stood there, wondering what to do. I watched the butterflies sitting on the purple creeping flower, opening and shutting their wings, and fiddling about with their whiskers. It could be nothing, an old bit of brass off a seed drill perhaps or a hedge-cutting tool? But I knew that wasn't. That was a woman's thing. I could tell that from the way that was twisted. As I scraped the dirt off with my nail I knew I'd got hold of some rare bit of history. Ah, I thought, you're romancing. But then I knew from what old Cave at school told us, I ought to take that to a museum. But if I telephoned what would they say? They'd just think I was a scruffy little old boy having them on: they might make out I'd stolen it. In any case, in order to get there I'd have to tell somebody. That was the real problem. Who was it to be? Suppose I told old Isaac? That was on his land after all. He'd just send old Abbs or Charlie out with a spade, and then what would happen? Old Charlie and Abbs seemed as honest as the day, but I didn't really know them, did I? Donald never said nothin' at all but just gave you a funny old secret look whatever you said. I didn't really know any of them. If old Mrs Walker got hold of it that would be all round Letheringsett and Holt in half a day: there'd be dozens up here. You can't tell with people you don't know like that, at least I couldn't. But then when I felt suspicious of them I felt bad, because the Walkers and old Abbs had been kind to me. I could have talked that over with my old Mum and Dad, but they were in Birmingham, for another ten days. In any case, I ought to be sure first. I ought to look round there a bit more to see if there was anything else, perhaps. If I just took that one thing along they'd laugh at me or take no notice. But how was I to be sure? If I was seen digging around or even hanging around that part, I would be noticed. Except, of course, they might think rabbits had gone to my head. I could be digging out rabbits ... I'd have to think that one out, too: so, I put the big pin back in the rabbit hole and marked the hole with a stick in the middle of the blue creeper. You have to think about this sort of thing very carefully, to make the right decisions. That took me twenty grass stems to suck, to think this one over, and even then I wasn't clear about what to do at all. I was really flummoxed.

Then I realised I'd have to write to old Cave. Only he'd think I was trying to make a fool of him, like I'd made a fool of myself in front of H.M. George VI.

I was well aware now of my two selves. There was the self that was the son of my father and my uncles, his brothers. They were real country larkers. Then there was the me with a bit of schooling: me with a little idea of study and what that meant. It wouldn't mean anything to these old country people. They had other skills and know-how: they were teaching me. But they hadn't a clue about old Cave's kind of knowledge and his respect for all that the British Museum meant to him. That great blackened building! It really frightened me, walking up those great big colonnades! What would it mean to old Charlie and old Abbs? As I thought about it, my mouth got tighter. I could just see them makin' a muck of it. Mind you, they kept saving me from danger and exhaustion, showing me how to hold a fork, and how not to stick it through my foot. They taught me how to do the things they could do. But they had a kind of pub justice about everything, and the Lord knows what kind of crazy kind of plan they'd make, if I showed them that torque and that really turned out to be gold! For one thing, they'd have all that hedge dug up before telling anyone else. I knew that was wrong, 'cause old Cave told us that when they dig things up they want to know exactly where that lay.

So, I had to spend the next two days working up and down that field, heaving up the sheaves, sometimes riding on the top of a load of corn, bouncing up and down on old Abbs' trailer, the shackles going a-chack-a-chack-a-chack behind the tractor, all along my hedge – and hardly daring to look at the warren.

'He want to see if he can get another rabbit,' said Charlie. 'You want to whistle to 'em boy, then they'll come out and eat out of yore hand. Heh! Heh!'

As soon as they were out of sight, I lay down and looked deep into that warren, into the holes where my find was. I found it again, and then poked around a bit with a stick to see what else there might be there. There wasn't anything for a bit, but then there was a little chinky noise. I put my hand down and felt something sharp, but when I got hold of it, that wouldn't move. What else was in there? I trembled and felt all peculiar. I had to do something now, that was certain. At first I thought of puttin' the torque in my pocket and runnin' home to old Isaac Walker. But then I thought I'll keep that quiet a little longer. Then I realised what was the best thing to do: I'd have a quiet word with my Uncle Tom, why ever didn't I think of that before? He had built the Shell Museum at Glandford and if he didn't know he could ask someone in Sir Alfred Jodrell's estate office.

SIX

The Shell Museum is down below the churchyard in the lane that runs down to the ford in Glandford. That was built by my Uncle Tom and his workmates for Sir Alfred in 1915. My Uncle showed me round one Sunday afternoon when we were down there. That was built partly of flint and partly of brick with a curvy round gable end like Home Farm, to fit in with the village, and Sir Alfred had all these here shells stored in boxes in Bayfield Hall. He'd collected them over sixty years all over the world. After they'd built the house for it, Uncle Tom fitted the museum out, with other carpenters makin' all the shelves and cases in there. He had spent the years 1896–1906 workin' on the renovation of St Martin's Church. Do you know, there's a little plaque on the wall of the vestry there, with his name on it among a list of all the craftsmen, for the work they did repairing all them screens and carvings? When I go in the church I think that's all a bit gloomy and old fashioned, and they've carved knots in everything in sight, only I know I couldn't do it, that was a real craft.

Old Sir Alfred and his sisters laid out all these shells along of my Uncle Tom. Of course, old Uncle Tom he never knew anything about shells or museums either, but he have a feeling for the sea seeing he live near Cley and Blakeney, and when you go into the museum that's like being at the bottom of the sea, and you might find mermaids in there. You go into that little old room at Glandford and that's full of pink and white light, just as if you were down at the bottom of a bit of clear sea in the sunlight, in the Mediterranean or somewhere. He painted that all white, with white showcases, and he fixed white scallop shells all up the beams and along. And then in the cases was laid out all the different kinds of shells found all over the world. You've never seen anything like it – big shells as large as cats, with spikes or ridges; some like big snails the size of rabbits with mother-of-pearl walls, all shiny with rainbow colours, perfect shapes like the horns of trumpets of tubes, little shells like jewels, white and pink.

There's orange and white carpet shells from Hunstanton beach and sun-ray shells from Florida, sharp-pointed shells from

Japan, pink-mouthed murex shells, and long conical twisted shells, that don't say where from. There's cephalopods and an Indian chank shell cut away to show the sort of spiral staircase inside. There's shell necklaces and coral necklaces, and big lumps of white coral. Two white fat sunfish hang over the cases of shells, and in them cases there's all kinds of other things besides, that people have sent – old stones and old-fashioned Victorian bits of this and that.

And up the end I saw some things that made me think now about my warren. There were some old glazed earthenware bottles they'd dug up in the village, just old brown bottles a couple of hundred years old, salt-glazed and a rum little shape. Here they were, kept because someone loved them. Come to think of it, the things I'd found were hundreds of times more interesting than these little old juggy bottles. Thinking about them, I could see now where my diggings fitted in, and how I ought to go to work. There was a bit of old Pompeii in there that was burned by a volcano and a sugar bowl used by old Queen Elizabeth and some jewels, and agate ware. And people sent all kinds of stuff to Tom, knowin' he'd take care of it.

The way old Uncle Tom laid that out, that wasn't just a job. You could see he was following an idea in his head. That's how Uncle Tom was different. Just as he could tell at a glance how many cubic feet of wood there was in a tree, so he worked his mind round everything, from the way to keep the stocks of trout up, to the names in the dog cemetery behind the Hall. He knew everything and he was always thinking about the millions of ways things can come into the world, and the difference in shapes and colours they take. I'd see him stroking long feathers out of a pheasant's tail wondering why the cocks had these long feathers, and one day he'd shown me a couple of young owl chicks out of a nest in a hollow tree up in Granny Bayfield's wood, when I come one weekend with my old Dad and Mum. They was funny fluffy little old white things with scrawny necks, not all round and big-headed like an old barn owl, old Billy Wix, at all. He was full of knowledge about nature, old Tom, and he'd suddenly come out with it. I was very shocked one day when he said to my old Dad, 'If a bulldog lay hold of somebody, do you know he won't let go?'

'Is that so?' said my old Dad.

'Do you know how to make him let go?'

'That I don't,' said Dad.

37

'You just want to stick your fingers up his back passage ... he'll let go then all right.'

My old Dad and Tom laughed.

'That's a masterpiece,' said my Dad.

I thought that was horrible. But that might be useful some day, and I never forgot it because that was a bit of biology, too, like all the other things Uncle Tom knew: how to get a ferret back out of a hole; how to keep rats inside your shirt (never leave one in there or he'll bite you – so long as there's two that's alright); how to castrate lambs with rubber bands: 'Carstrate' he called that.

But the Shell Museum, that was really out of Tom's head, like the marquetry patterns on the altar top. Do you know, when he was doin' the renovations he used only olive wood? He got that out of the ends of orange boxes from Jerusalem so that would be the right kind of thing from the Holy Land, to suit the richest part of the job.

Uncle Tom was the one! That wasn't any good trustin' anyone else with the story of my diggings: only Tom would appreciate that what was important was to recognise that, in fumblin' about and uncovering that gold piece, I had touched the hands of people who lived hundreds and hundreds of years ago. If I put the ordinary old country people in touch with it, they'd do something wrong because they didn't have the kind of understanding Uncle Tom had gained. Even old Isaac, like as not, would start draggin' out the hedge with a cable and claw, and get a tractor to dig it. Charlie and Abbs would get shovels and then half the village would come along, and pick up whatever bits they could. I'd read about all that in my Children's Encyclopaedia, how thieves had ransacked old tombs, all through the ages. I'd read about that old Viking ship, found in 1904 at Oseberg in Norway: the burial chamber had been stripped just after that was buried, and they'd even wrenched the arms and hands off Queen Asa, to get at her rings and her golden bracelets. That was in 870 AD, but there were old boys then like some of them in my school who'd nick anything they could lay their hands on. And in Egypt, and Italy, the old robbers were still at work on the tombs and treasures, as old Cave had told us. He used to spend his holidays digging on these sites sometimes.

One day, that little old piece I'd found might lie in the British Museum, too, in the show cases, and people might come from all over the world to look at it, and study it. Perhaps they might say, 'Found by a schoolboy at Letheringsett in 1938.'

Was it Anglo-Saxon? Every time I said one of those words to myself, I felt a little old thrill in my guts. People could go and study them things for ever, near as damn it. Perhaps what I had touched down there would alter everything we knew about the people who left them there, how they ate, what weapons they had, what tools they used to harvest their crops and catch their old rabbits.

Of course, I could get excited about old Abbs' eujackapivvies for his carts, about how to stook and cart corn, and how to kill a rabbit. But I could get more excited, like old Tom could, about things like those in my diggings that stick up out of history. I must go to Uncle Tom at once, I felt sure. Only I don't like rushin' into decisions. I said to myself, I'll give that two days and then if I still think that's right I'll go up to the Reading Room.

The Gates of Bayfield Hall

SEVEN

Next evening, Isaac Walker and me, we went shooting rats in the big barn. The farmer said he was sick of them: they'd spoilt a whole sack of cattle cake, and they didn't seem to be affected by the poison he put down, some nasty old blue paste. He had a .410 shotgun. That wouldn't do much damage to the barn walls, but he said I weren't to fire at the roof.

'Am I going to fire that, then?' I exclaimed.

'Your eyes are quicker nor mine, boy. Have you ever fired a gun?'

'Oh, yes,' I said. That wasn't true. I'd shot an airgun, but that only went phut. I couldn't think what happened when you fired a shotgun that went off with gunpowder and kicked. I couldn't wait for that to get dark.

Mr Walker opened the barn door very quietly: he simply let it off its string. The farmer had a long battery torch: at once he shone the beam along the main beam on the opposite wall, and there was a rat, black, with light in its eyes, scuttling along to get out of sight.

I looked along the barrel, held the gun somehow and fired. The whole barn was full of the smart, sharp noise and brick dust puffed into the beams of the torch. And so did the rat. That leapt into the air with a bloody mark on its shoulder and dived to the floor with a slumpy noise. My mouth felt dry and my heart beat. The old farmer laughed and patted me in a teasing sort of way, only I could see he was pleased, too.

'Ho! Ho! Talk about beginner's luck! Well done, boy. Tha's another bugger that won't eat no more of my feed. Now we'll try the stackyard.'

There was nothing in the stackyard: I expect the other rats had heard the shot and fled. So we waited in the dark for a bit, listening. I could feel the tingling warmth of my feet in the rubber boots and smell the strong smell of dung, a reek like ammonia catching in my breath from time to time.Then we heard a little noise at the hen house, a queer little skirl of protest from a hen, then bump bump down the run. Mr Walker switched on the torch. And there was something I'd never seen before. There were two rats. One was on his back holding an egg in his legs, and the other was pulling him by the tail down the walkway: Mrs Walker had left the little flap up.

'Go on, blast, boy,' yelled the farmer. 'Shoot the bors!'

But I was so surprised, I hadn't even cocked the gun: I pulled the trigger and nothing happened.

'Hold on! … Don't you shoot me!' cried old Isaac, and he came down with a crack on one of the rats with an iron bar he'd snatched up from the side of the barn. The other rat got away underneath the hen house and we fired a few shots under there, but got nothing. The old hens went silly, squawking and caterwauling. But the rat Mr Walker hit was all jammy with its insides splashed all around, so that was a score of two. We were quite pleased with ourselves.

That gave me an idea. I said to Mr Walker, 'Can I use that gun in your fields?'

'So long as you don't shoot any game, boy. Don't let me see you taking a pot shot at any of them old pheasants or partridges. Tha's out o' season, anyway. That old pheasant the other day, we shan't say nothing about him 'cause he got caught in the binder. Nor them old hares, 'cause that was harvest home and that count as ground game. But rabbits and pidgeons, and any old rats you can see … but do you take care boy,' he said, looking a bit thoughtful. 'Carry your gun like this, always pointed to the ground. Don't load it while you're on the highway. And don't cock it till you're stalking. When you go through a hedge or climb over a gate, take that cartridge right out, in case you fall soshways acrorst a root, or catch your sleeve on something. Don't poke that in the earth either, do you'll get the ind full o' muck or that'll burst when you fire off. We don't want no dead boys: them buggers are enough of a bloody nuisance alive – when they're dead you have to carry the bors everywhere…' And he showed his funny old green teeth and gave one of his 'har har's.

He made me repeat all these instructions. But now, you see, I could go digging in that field up by the wood and make out I was digging out rabbits, with a gun ready making it look clear enough what I was doing. Nobody would suspect me of rooting for treasure, 'cause they'd think I was rabbiting.

Old Mrs Walker, she didn't seem to be able to accept I was old enough to take a gun out.

'Well, if that was me,' she said to old Isaac, 'he shouldn't hev it for nobody. He'll go a-splodden over some slushy pightle and

41

lump into a grup with a jilk, then that tarnation thing'll go off. He'll get his face skint or his brains blowed out or suthen, and sarve you right, that'll learn him perhaps!'

'Ah,' said Isaac laconically. 'Tha's very likely! If you keep a-mobbin'.'

'Ah!' she said. 'That may be all very well, but that kind o' thing do torment my insides so.'

Then she did a funny thing: she looked him hard in the face and cried out in a singsongy sort of voice: 'And the Lord commandeth the angel: and he put up his sword again in the sheath thereof!'

This was a new side to Mrs.

EIGHT

Now, what I don't like in life is nasty surprises. But they do come. The next evening I was sitting on the bank up by my digging, havin' a bit of a think again. I was just goin' to have a scratch around when I saw three boys walkin' up the side of the field. I didn't want them to start a-wonderin' what I was up there for, so I fired a shot into the hedge to make out I was after rabbits. Then I waved: but they didn't wave back, so I said to myself hullo, that's a bit rum.

As they got nearer, I could see they were the old boys who were running about in the harvest field after the rabbits. There was Bob, who was about fifteen, Roger, who was about fourteen, and Tim, who was younger. They wore grey flannel shirts, open at the neck. Bob and Roger wore braces and corduroy trousers, and Tim had grey flannel ones with a belt. But their faces didn't look right, somehow.

'Hullo,' I said, standing there as they walked up. But they didn't reply. Instead, Bob came straight up to me, drew his arm back and punched me in the face. His fist caught me on the side of the cheek and crunched hard into my head! Oh, his bony old hand was hard! I went all dizzy, because I didn't expect that. The others bent down and grabbed sods off the bank and threw them into my face.

I struck out and hit Bob's shoulder, but that was a soft blow and had no force in it. It made him catch his breath, though.

'Tha's for pickin' the best rabbits and givin' me a mucky old milky doe,' gasped Bob.

'Ah!' said Tim. 'Comin' up here and takin' all the best stuff just 'cause you're a-stayin' with old Isaac Walker. You want to watch your step, city kid!'

I was still thrown right out with surprise, so I still didn't know what to say, and while I tried to get my breath Roger came up to me, and pushed me into the hedge. It was a prickly hawthorn hedge and there seemed to be about a thousand thorns sticking in my back. Then they all threw some more sods at me, blinding me, all the earth going in my mouth, and ran off.

I'm sorry to say I blubbered, because it was a rotten trick taking me off my guard like that. But then I went into a blind rage. I didn't know what I was doing, but I went all electric all over and my heart beat hard. There was a black kind of explosion in my head. I dug my feet into the warren holes in the bank and tore myself out of that hedge. I could hear my jacket ripping on a branch. And then I got up, picked up a big sod of earth and threw it at one of them, just before they got out of reach. I didn't know that at the time, but that had a big flint inside, and this hit Tim square on the back of the head. He fell down, clutchin' his hands to his head, and the others stopped runnin', and came back to him. I could see blood run over his fingers, and he looked ever so white, I could see that from twenty yards away. He began to whine, and I stood stock still.

'You've killed him!' shouted Bob, who had a face with big bones in it, a real country face. 'You broke his bloody hid you hev. You'll get paid out for that!'

'Ah, go to hell,' I panted. I started to sneak away. I didn't like myself for that. But there was three of them. And I was fed up, to be drawn into all this animal rage, when I had so much else to think about.

There was so much blood, they got frightened. They went quiet. One of them put his handkerchief under Tim's head to staunch the flow and they lifted him up, and helped him stumbling down the field. I turned and looked, feeling all cold and watery in my legs, and just wished that all hadn't happened. Then I made off, gasping and panting, across the stubble field to the farm. I was glad I'd got away and that I'd managed to take the gun with me. I stopped and took the cartridge out. You shouldn't ever run with a gun loaded, Isaac had told me.

Roger saw me runnin' home and, lookin' back, shouted, 'You wait till we tell old Walker! You'll have the coppers on your trail ... City kid!' Then I lost sight of them. But then that struck me that might be serious, and I ran like I've never run before, back to the farm. When I got there I was pantin' and groanin', and the first one I run into was old Abbs. Comin' round the corner of the flint wall I ran straight into his fat old stomach with my head down and dropped the gun. He gasped.

'Blast, boy, you'd kill anybody, drivin' round the corner like that. Bless my heart alive ... Hum ... hoogh!'

'I ... I think I have killed somebody,' I panted.

'Ouch, bloody hell, boy, what are you a-tellin' us? Oh, hum ... hoogh ... bloody boys is allus in trouble when they aren't at work. Blast, you fare t'lay me low ... Ough!'

'I threw a lump of earth at a boy and that had a stone in it ...' I sobbed. I was blubberin' now. I picked the gun up.

'You better come an' see Isaac,' grumbled old Abbs. 'Here I am on the way to the pub for a wet and blast here's this here boy cannonin' round like a bloody bull what have got bot-fly. Phin ... phin ...'

'I'm sorry Mr Walker,' I said. 'I think I've killed a boy.'

The farmer turned pale under his dark beard stubble.

'If you have, boy, you'll be worse than sorry. I hope that weren't with my gun?' Course, that weren't legal for a boy of fifteen to carry a shotgun, if he was found out.

I said I did fire at a rabbit, but that was before the boys arrived. He looked a little relieved, but not much. He wasn't sure whether to believe me. My heart was sinking, because now I had to work out who I could trust and also who would believe what I said – here I was getting into a state of affairs in Glandford neighbourhood where no one would believe a word I said.

'I was sitting up there in the field and three boys come up ...' They were the boys who were in the harvest field ...'

'Old Lightfoot's boys, I'll lay a bob,' said old Abbs. 'They're always looking for trouble. Ha ... humph ...' He fair rumbled down in his chest.

'Careful now, Albert,' said Isaac. 'You want to be careful what you say on account o' the law. Just let him tell his story.'

My sweat was beginning to drag now and I felt all cold with fear. I didn't like that word 'law'. Would I have to answer a lot of questions like what I was doing in that field?

'They come up to me and I said "Hullo", but they didn't say nothing. The big one, Bob, he hit me in the face. He never said nothin' first.'

'Tha's true: tha's bruised on his right cheek,' said Albert Abbs. 'Tha's a rum go that is, hum!'

'Then the others threw lumps o' muck at me all in my face. And that one called Roger run up and pushed me into the hedge.'

'Bloody old boys!' said old Abbs, who couldn't help himself.

'So when I got up I was ever so angry and I threw a lump of earth at them, and that hit that one called Tim. There must have been

45

a stone in my sod, because that cut his head and made that bleed.'

Mr Walker took that all in and he rubbed his chin.

'They set on you like that, without givin' you a chance to put your hands up, three against one?'

'Yes,' I said, with a choke.

'And threw sods into your face?'

For answers I gave a nod and a kind of whine.

'Albert, do you think you could go round there on the tractor and see how bad that boy is?'

'There aren't no lights on the tractor 'cause we took them off when we built the trailer. But I'll go if I can have your car.'

'I don't want to go myself because this here boy is in my charge and you're a bit more impartial as a third party, if you don't mind.'

'Mind? Well–hum–that's goodbye to my pint, I dare say. Never mind – that never rain but that pour. Phin! Why don't they put all old boys in a home or sothen?'

So old Abbs went off to the boy's home and I sat with Mr Walker in his parlour, with a grandfather clock tickin' slowly away. I was all cold now and shakin', and thought perhaps he'd send me home to Norwich. Then what should I do about my find? I reckon I'd have to abandon that altogether.

That seemed everything was against me. Now there could even be police looking into that and they'd want to find the stone that cut Tim's head, and be routing around. Or if I went up there, I'd be suspected of trying to hide evidence, or the boys'd come up and beat me up again. And who would believe me now? At the thought of my disgrace, I broke out in a whimpery sniffle again.

'Don't take on so,' said old Isaac kindly. 'Let's hope that in't too bad.' He bared his rickety old teeth at me and gave me a kind of weak smile.

'Always into trouble at your age. Mind you,' he added, 'that could be very bad. Don't you ever get your rag out like that again.'

We heard old Abbs come back in the farmer's little old Ford Saloon. He came in looking relieved.

'Tha's a nasty cut,' he said. 'Only tha's only superfixial. That was a sharp little flint, only that was all surrounded by earth and that. So long as he don't go gangrene or lockjaw, or some bloody compilation. Hum! ... 'Cause if he do he'll have to have his head cut off.' Old Abbs grabbed Isaac's shoulder, in relief, and laughed.

'Old Lightfoot he started sayin' "that little bugger fired his gun at them". I said, "Tha's bloody romentin' for a start 'cause he shot at a rabbit afore them old boys was anywhere near him."'

'Well, he han't got no rabbit to show for it,' said Isaac.

'Old Lightfoot, blast he were in a state. "Any old how," he say, "I'll have the law on the little bugger all the same." I say to him "How bad is that?" "Well," he say, "now I've washed his bloody head under the pump, that en't all that bad." "Well," I said, "I'll tell you suffin. Your boys harboured some grievance against Duffy Ransome on account of a milky doe they thought he swung on 'em. They went straight up to him and swiped him in the kisser without saying one word o' warnin'. Only he didn't know nothing about the milky doe, 'cause I work with that boy, and I know what he know and what he don't know. Ough ... hum ... An' he never said, 'Oh, I fobbed them off with an old milky doe, nor nothing'. And next day I heared him ask old Charlie Bacon what a milky doe were. He wanted a sartain rabbit because he killed that himself and that was the first thing he'd ever killed – I knew that. Only they never give him no chance t'explain."'

I was really feeling relief now, because I didn't realise till now how much old Abbs understood about me. He was after justice, even though I hadn't been very just in my thoughts about him.

'An' I said to old Lightfoot, "I know that boy and how he don't tell bloody hummers, sartainly not when he's in the state he's in now with his face all bruised." And I told him how Roger punch him in the face, then Bob and Tim started throwing sods in his eyes. They didn't deny it. "If your bloody old boys," I said, "behave like that, all accounts of a bloody rabbit dinner, hum ... hum ... then they deserve to get hurt."'

He was really out of breath now coughing and phumin' like an old engine. I couldn't stop a shiver, this time from relief

'"Is that true?" old Lightfoot say. One of them old boys nodded, sulky he was. "Shut up!" said one of the others. "We'll get him for this," said the other ... Hough! ... So I said, "Now look you here – you got away with this here. If you want a rabbit, you come and ask me, but you leave that boy alone. If you do anything to him, you won't just have his bad temper to deal with – hum! ... You'll have me to deal with and then you'll get a fair thackin'."'

Old Abbs shook his head. I didn't know what to say.

'I'm sorry for what I did,' I said feebly.

47

'You mustn't lose control of yourself like that, boy,' said old Isaac, 'but I think tha's a rum un, when they make three agin one like that, wicked ol' boys!'

'About nawthin',' said old Abbs. 'I can tell you what that was really about. He's a stranger. Tha's what that is. He come from Norwich. He don't belong to Letheringsett. He's "City"! Tha's all that is. They'd have found some excuse for goin' for him, any old road. Hum! ... I'm goin' to have my pint now at last, up the Bell ... Dawg eat ber-loody dawg, that's what they say ... hoogh!'

He shook his head vigorously, his fat cheeks wobbling, and gasping in his tubes. But I was relieved by the way he and Isaac had sorted that out: they were really wanting to be fair to everyone. I was miserable, though, to give Isaac all that trouble and I was in a bigger mess than ever over my bit of history.

The trouble was, word of all this'd get to my Uncle Tom, I knew, before I went to him, and if I was going to confide in him I'd have to be in his good books.

Of course, Mrs was on about that was what she expect, sending a boy off with a gun like that, though that was nothing to do with a gun, and how she'd have 'given me a rare twiltin' if I'd have been her boy, traipsin' the field kickin' up a stive with everyone and chelpin' everyone and gettin' a smack aside of the lug like I deserved'.

At last old Isaac took out his pipe and say to her, 'Why maw, for the Lord's sake leave off a crackin' o' your jaw, and get up timber hill.'

And so, of course, I had to go to bed, too. So I didn't have no chance to see my Uncle that night and no doubt he'd hear about all that in Wiverton Blue Bell that night.

48

NINE

'Upaday!' old Charlie Bacon said next morning, as we were getting up towards the top of the first stack, 'I'ouldn't like to be in your shoes when you come acrorst your Uncle Tom next.'

'Like as not,' said old Abbs, 'he'll swipe you one acrost the lug an' all.'

My heart sank. It was as I feared.

'We was all up the Bell last night when your Uncle come in. Well, you know, they all respect old Tom: only he's a gentleman's man, with the game to look after and the old gentry's park. He's a good old boy. But if they get a chance to put one over on him, Lord, they'll all rise to that, round here.'

And I had given them a chance.

Old Charlie was as lively as a button: he loved a good story. He turned over a few sheaves and tossed them into place.

'Old Lightfoot was there and he made that up into a tidy little story time he'd finished. "That little bugger picked up this here great rock and threw that with all his might: he didn't have no regard for life nor limb," he said.'

'That's not true,' I said.

'Tha's what old Abbs say, but then Lightfoot say, "Who's word do you take? Tha's only his word against mine. All I know is my little Tim have got a hool in his head big as a ring ousel's egg."'

'Your Uncle stood there and his whiskers twitched like old Tom Tit Tot's, hum ... hum ...' said old Abbs. 'Only I noticed that when I put in a word for you against Lightfoot's, his old ears were right out on stalks.'

'There's one who won't believe what they say about you,' said Charlie, leapin' to the end of the stack.

'Who's that?' I asked, my heart leaping.

'Your old Aunt Anna,' and old Charlie Bacon kissed the back of his hand.

'Yew soft old bugger!' said Abbs, scathingly. And to me he added, 'Blast, Charlie think she's the most wonderful woman in the world ... Humph!'

Old Charlie Bacon blushed, under his ancient crinkled skin, and went thoughtful.

'Hum! ...' added old Abbs, thoughtful. 'If she asked him to turn over every pebble on Cley beach he'd do it for her.'

'She's a good cook,' I said.

'She's the kindest old woman I've ever known,' said Charlie. 'Why, before my old mother died – she was ninety-six – we kept a-strugglin' to keep the poor old mawther reasonable – she was incontinent. Well, there was only me and my old sister, she's a right fule. Well, your old Anna used to go there every other day to change her like a baby, and she'd scrub up and that ... wonderful.'

The old man leaned his fork against himself and got his red spotted handkerchief out, and wiped his eyes. He was letting out great big tears, about my Aunt Anna. I felt all solemn, because I loved my old Aunt, but that made me go all queer to see this old man pipe his eye about her.

'Then she died,' he said, fumbling with his hanky. 'Fortunately, she went quick and quiet. I hope I go like it.'

'Hum ...,' said old Abbs in his chest.

'What's incontinent?' I asked.

'When you get old, you get like a baby, that is, if you're lucky ... hough ...' said old Abbs.

'You do it in your pants,' said old Charlie.

I never knew that about old people.

'Well, now and then, you know,' added Charlie, 'she just needed lookin' after, you know. She weren't datty, not really datty. Only your old Auntie she did what none of us liked doin', if Betty had an accident.'

He got down off the stack to do what he called a Jimmy Riddle in the hedge. Old Abbs joined him and I went on the end of the line. That's funny how, on a job, men all go in the hedge at once. Mostly people don't notice these things, but you do when you're an old boy. And I was proud to be standing there on the end of the line against the hedge with the men. That's funny, isn't it?

Anyway, we all seemed ever so close to one another that day, because of old Charlie and the way he loved Aunt Anna. We heard some more about it at fourses, that is dinner time: besides washing old Betty Bacon, Aunt Anna used to take her meals and bread.

'She's a Christian, she is,' said Charlie. 'Old Tom, he's a churchwarden, and he do all the work in the church.'

50

They got on about Uncle Tom's altar top, and how he made that out of olive wood from crates from Palestine. Old Abbs said old Tom, he felt he had a special privilege from the Almighty.

'Some woman put an altar cloth over that table one day an' old Tom whipped that off. "Fancy puttin' that bloody thing over my altar",Tom said. Oh! Phum!'

Old Abbs choked and laughed, 'I thought he was goin' to have a fit like that 'leptic boy at school who foam at the mouth once a term.'

'But she do the Christian works, boy,' said Charlie. 'She in't afraid o' nawthin'. An' Tom's the same!'

'Have you seen his tools?' asked old Abbs.

I shook my head.

'Hum ... hoogh! ... You ought to see 'em – rabbiting planes, mould-cutting planes, some on 'em have got the rummest names – fillister, old woman's tooth! Ough! Marvellous stuff. He molly-coddle them there little old eujackapivvies like as if they was rare bantams or Chinese fantails, boy. He have them lyin' in boxes, all sharpened up, ready.'

I sighed.

'Clean, dry and slightly oiled, like guns in the Army,' he added.

'You're right an' all,' said Charlie Bacon. 'They're good people, old Tom an' Anna. Why, sometimes you feel nowadays there's nivver nobody about to help nobody with nawthin. But old Tom an' Anna, they aren't like that at all!'

So they went on all day, ruminating about my aunt and uncle, especially Charlie. Well, anyway, at last that next field was all done and all the shooves were in stacks, and we went off riding on the trailer as old Abbs drove that off, back down the farm.

I was so thoughtful all through tea, old Isaac and his missus kept a-lookin' at me curious. Eventually Mrs Walker, she couldn't stand that no longer.

'That boy's wholly quiet,' she said, nodding at me. 'Is any-thing wrong?'

Old Isaac showed his funny old teeth, grinnin' at me.

'He's romentin', I reckon,' he said.

'Romentin'', that mean romancing, makin' up hummers in your head. I said I weren't romenting.

'I think I'd like to go and see my Uncle Tom,' I said.

'Ah,' said Isaac. 'No doubt you want to git that straight with him, that stive you kicked up along o' them boys. Well, do you go up there and have that all out with old Tom and Anna. Otherwise they're goin' to git hold o' that by hearsay and get in a right passe about that.'

So, I tidied myself up a bit and set off up the road. Now, would you believe it, my Uncle Tom set off just about that minute, to walk down to Letheringsett to see me, or so I reckon. I reckon someone had put a tizzy on my Uncle Tom over me since I had this thing to tell him. Everything went wrong. I needed to get across to him, but every time I tried, something went duzzy.

Whenever I got into trouble, my uncle's face seemed to come through the hedge or corner of the wood, with his cap and his waxed up whiskers, just at the wrong moment.

The first time was on this same evening, just as I got passed our field, about a mile up the hill from Isaac's farm. Along come an old bread van, tearing home at the end of the day. Well, just as he come over a little hump, the driver was looking at me. He didn't see an old pheasant run out of the verges on the other side of the road. That flew against the side of his van and that went 'bang' against the side, just about fifty feet of me. Ho, I thought, that's dead as a door-nail; I'll take that to my Uncle Tom. He'll know what that's right to do with a dead pheasant.

Well, I didn't know, but these old birds, if they get a knock and that don't kill 'em, they faint. They'll lie down like as if they're dead with their eyes closed. But if you get near 'em they'll suddenly squawk and jump up, and run off like clockwork. Well, anyway, I ran up, this old cock pheasant jumped up: but I was excited now and didn't think anymore. I just fell on him and picked him up by the legs, and twisted his neck. I'd seen old Abbs do that to the pheasant that got cut up by the binder in the harvest field, and afterwards he'd shown me how to do it. He let me practise that a bit, so that I could do it quickly.

'You don't want to mess about,' he said, 'otherwise the poor buggers suffer.'

So, I give that old run-over pheasant a wring and that worked. He was dead, though of course, his wings kept on flapping a bit with the life in his nerves. Just as he was a-doin' this, Uncle Tom come over the rise. He hadn't seen the van, not to notice. All he saw was his nephew with a pheasant and that was flapping in its death throes in my hand.

52

It would be beyond me to describe Uncle Tom's face. That was like thunder. He let out such a duller, you'd think he was the Almighty catchin' Adam eatin' that apple. He shook his stick somethin' terrible, and he was after me, his old boots comin' clitter clatter down the road; who could have stood their ground in the face of that? Any old how, I was off. I reckoned he'd be on to me with that old stick afore I'd got a word out about how I was puttin' the poor thing out of its misery.

Old Tom, no doubt he could catch men poachers, but he couldn't get me. First I flung that old cock pheasant over the flint wall and then I dodged into the wood. I had in mind a set of big holes I'd seen under a beech tree. I reckon they were badger holes. I'd been mucking about in there, and I'd tried to get in them, to see if I could see any old badgers down there. There was a bit of old grass and leaves and stuff, all swept out, and all around the holes the dirt was swept clean. I got down in one o' them holes and swept that clean outside with my arm, so that didn't show no footmarks. I was all of a muckwash by now, behind a thorny gorse bush. I tried to stop breathing hard, in case he heard me wheezing.

Anyhow, I heard old Tom crashing about and talking to himself. 'He's just like his father and his brothers ... allus after the game ... Mind you,' he panted, 'I never caught them red-handed ... not like this one ... Anna, my dear, I reckon you're wrong ... She keep standin' up for him ... I'm right an' all ... I'll tell her so when I git home ... that bloody old boy's a poacher, as sure as eggs is eggs, like his father, 'cause now I seen him doin' it ... in broad daylight, on the King's highway an' all!'

I sat there a long time, the cold sweat drying on me, after he'd gone away, muttering and shaking his stick like fury.

TEN

So, I was mortal careful not to meet my Uncle Tom that evening. I thought I'd better make myself scarce an' all, in case he come down to old Isaac Walker's farm to enquire after me. That was a fine cool evening. So, I walked up to the village and on to Wiverton, and then Blakeney: that was about three miles. In Blakeney, I found a fish and chip shop that was frying, and bought myself six pennorth of fish and chips. I shook some salt on my packet out of a big aluminium salt pot, and sat and ate them in the shop where that was warm with the heat of the fryer. The frying machine was run on coal and was all smart with white tiles with a lighthouse design in the middle of the back wall. They were good chips, nice and firm – I don't like the sort that go all greasy and limp. That fish was really fresh, a bit of rock salmon with good crisp batter on it. When I'd done I wiped my fingers on the newspaper they were wrapped in and set off back to Wiverton. That was gettin' dark now and a bit breezy, and the tall hedges were rocking about a bit. It was a bit creepy in the lanes.

At Wiverton was the public house where they all went, called the Bell. That was the Blue Bell really, only they called it just the Bell. The fish and chips had made me thirsty and that got something terrible time I had walked along that country lane for a mile from Blakeney to Wiverton. I was too young to go into the pub, so I tapped on the door at the back and asked if I could have a lemonade outside in the yard: so the landlord brought me one in a glass and I stood outside drinking it, on the doorstep among the empty beer crates, and that. My old Dad, he'd given me a half a crown for spending money for three weeks and I had half of it left.

Now I could hear people talking in the Public Bar. I don't usually hang about trying to overhear what other people are saying, but I was trying to make out if my Uncle Tom was in there because, if he was, I thought I'd better clear out quick. The old landlord and his missus were having a bit of an argument about the big clock in the bar. He was being a bit stubborn, I reckon, just out of cussedness, and she kept on at him.

'Do you wind that clock,' she said, 'don't that'll stop.'

'Do that stop,' he replied, 'we can go on servin' people and make a bit more money overtime,' he said.

'Tha's right, John,' said someone. 'Do you let the bugger stop do we can be here all night.'

Anyway, he must have got a key because I could hear him working on the old clock; that made a noise like a dog snarling as he wound it up.

'Don't you overwind that, do that'll break,' his old woman said. He didn't seem to do nothin' right where she was concerned.

'Ha' you got any cheroots?' someone asked. 'I went to see old Roger ... he's laid up convalescin'. He said he'd love a cheroot.'

'No, that I han't,' said the landlord, closing the clock case. 'Tha's a rum un, you should ask. T'ain't often but what I always have some. But I han't got a bugger on the place.'

'Old Roger ...?' said another voice. 'Whoi, Harreh, was that some relation o' yours?'

'Noo,' the voice replied, 'oonly brother.'

That was all very confusin', tryin' to follow them, even in ordinary talk. When they started fooling, that was even worse.

Suddenly I heard a voice I knew.

'How are you then, altogether ... Humph?' Old Abbs must have come rolling in.

'Blast, tha's old Abbs! What are you goin' to have, bor?'

'I'll have a pint o' half-and-half if you're distributin' largers, Harreh.'

'I see you're a-gettin' on well with that barleh along the road there.'

'Cheero, bor. Tha's a-comin' up nice. Humph ...'

I could hear a windy, gurglin' sound as half that pint went down old Abbs' gullet.

'Tha's dusty that old barley, though. That do seem datty this year. I reckon when that get in the mill, in the troshin', they'll be some muck flyin' about.'

'Did that tempest lodge a lot on it?'

'Noo, we'd got that all up afore that come down. And that drain away quick up there.'

'Blast, there's a sight o' sluss in the field across the road here. That all ran down off the Downs, do you can't hardly get a cart along the drift.'

55

'Tha's a wittery little old crop old Blowers got off o' there any old road.'

'He got some tidy old crops up towards Letheringsett.'

There was a pause.

'How's that old boy gettin' on, workin' alongside you, Albert?'

'He's all right. He was pamplin' at it a bit when he started, 'fraid to get his feet datty. Phumph! But he soon got into it. He do a good day's work for a younker now.'

I glowed, to hear such praise.

'Course, tha's only temporary: he's here on holiday, so a lot o' the time he's just pruggin' about.'

'Ah.'

There was a pause while they thought.

'He do blee his old Dad.'

'Do he though?'

'Spit image of Ken.'

'An' in his way o' goin' on, too, little bit they do say.'

That set old Abbs wheezin'. 'Phumph! Ough! How do you mean, bor?'

'His old dad could knock a few things over on the quiet ...'

'He'd ... hum ... huddle a rabbit or two now or then, doubtless.'

'Ah. He'd have more 'n that.'

'I seen him hangin' round Bayfield lake.'

'Well, what do that prove?'

'Ah, some of them can tickle up a dinner or two an' all.'

'Like father, like son, I say.'

'Humph! He know sawthin', don't he!' said Abbs, scathingly, waggin' his head at the others, I bet.

'Wha's he a-doin' up there then, night after night, along the hedge of that field where you're a workin'?'

'I han't seen him.'

'I hev. He's after sawthin' up there, I'll be bound,' said the one they call Harry. 'I go up to Letheringsett to see my sister every evenin' arter work, an' every evenin' that old boy ha' been up there. I seen him scutterin' about up and down that bank, and I said to myself I bet that old boy is settin' snares or puttin' down raisins soaked in rum or sawthin'....'

'Humph!' exclaimed Abbs. 'I never heard such a load of old

56

gammarattle in my life. Any road, if anyone come by sawthin' on the side, good luck to 'em, I say.'

'His old Uncle Tom don't think that.'

'Tha's different. Tha's his livelihood, keeping the game. Apart from him, there an't many of us don't do a bit o' snaring or clouting some old cock pheasant a-sittin' up there in a bush at night, I'll be bound ...'

'Ah,' they all said. There was a pause while they all thought about poaching and what they should say next. They were careful they weren't going to give themselves away.

'That old chapel preacher over at Hunworth, they say, he ha' come out strong against poachin'.'

'Go to hell!' said Harry. 'He's one ter talk.'

'He's a right old dumplin'-hunter he is,' agreed old Abbs. 'He's lookin for some old chapel-gooin' farmer to give him a good meal, I reckon. Humph! Blast! Time he's a-huckerin' about a few bloody old birds he want to tell them to give the men who work for him a few more bob for a day's work. What the hell have a bit of poachin' to do with religion?'

'Th'Almighty put 'em there for all of us, didn't 'e?' said Harry. 'Tha's right!'

'My motto,' said Harry. 'That is ... that if you can get away with it ... findin's keepin's! I know if one wander into my garden he on't walk out agin!'

'Ah!' they all said. 'Tha's right an' all.'

'Tha's a pity we can't eat hod-a-ma-dods,' said someone.

They laughed. 'Them old Froggies do,' said an old man. 'I seen 'em in the war.'

'See old Abbs at it, like an old mavish peckin' a dodman!'

While they were gaspin' and laughin', I cleared off. I didn't understand all of it, but I'd heard enough to understand that everyone was suspicious of me, so I'd have to be careful. And I could tell that if any of them found anything, the one thing they'd want to do would be to make off with it and sell it, or something silly. There was only one person now who wouldn't make a mess of it – and that was my Uncle Tom. I must get through to him somehow, though somehow, I knew, my luck was against it.

Meanwhile, I wrote to old Cave.

ELEVEN

Home Farm
Letheringsett
25th August 1938

Dear Mr Cave,

I hope you aren't in Egypt as I am writing about something urgent. I am here for my health. I have been harvesting. In a field I found a gold circle in the ground that looks like one of the torcques we saw (Anglo-Saxon) in the London Museum. I hope you don't think I'm a lyiar since the City Hall business. I never meant to get on the wrong side of you as I like History. This find is historical.

Yours faithfully

R. Ransome

TWELVE

The second time old Tom come across me in a rum go was the very next day. I took a day off: old Isaac didn't mind. He never expected me to work all the time. I thought I might go back and do a bit of hay-raking with Donald and his horse round the field in the afternoon. I was sitting by the river near Glandford Ford, just day-dreaming. That was a sunny afternoon and I sat on a grassy bank, just looking at everything. The water sparkled very bright and clear, and in it I could see, every now and then, shoals of little fish, minnows, I suppose, mud-coloured, and stripey. Every now and then, when they'd all be pointed one way, say with their noses down to the left, they'd all suddenly change direction, with their noses up to the right. They'd all flick at once into this new position, and I wondered how they did it. You know what that's like on a field with boys doing physical excercises: how do you get them all to stand on their heads at once? That take weeks to get that all together, otherwise you have one standing on his head and another just getting down on his hands, and one just coming down all higgeldy-piggeldy. All these little fish went round twenty degrees together, whiz whiz – quicker nor you looked. And I wondered how that was done. I've seen it with pigeons, flying round from a loft. All of a sudden, they fly round and then sweep back in a different curve, up they go, and down they dip – all keeping just the right distance between one another. How do they do that? Perhaps they go into a kind of trance, so they all think together? Anyhow, that beat me. They don't have no wireless, anyhow, we know. So that's a mystery.

On the surface of the water there was flying bright blue dragonflies, like thin little hair pins of blue fire. There were some yellow flags by the bank, in full flower with dark green leaves shaped like swords. Right on the surface, bending the skin of the water, were water-boatman insects, moving up and down. I had my nose close to the water, you see, and I could see all sorts, even fresh water shrimps down the bottom, now and then, making a little puff of mud as they skimmed along among the green weed that looked like rhubarb, only more floppy and green.

I woke up out of this day-dreaming to hear a kind of squawking and choking sound. I couldn't make that out at first, but then across on the other side, lower down, I saw a dirty old angry swan. Now you expect a swan to look the most beautiful thing of all with his long curvy neck and to behave like that's in some fairy story, like some prince who's got bewitched, or something. But this here swan wasn't: that was trying to kill a duck. It had this duck by the neck in its beak, and its feathers were all fluffed up in a rage, and that kept holding this poor duck under the water, so the duck was all black mud, and the swan's head and neck were all black, too. I suppose that duck had swum into the swan's bit of river what he reckoned was his property or something. But that wasn't trying to drown it in clear water, that dirty old swan was holding it down in this here black mud and you could see by the look in that swan's eye that had got murder in his mind.

I felt horrible because that seemed so mean and cruel, whether that was natural or not. That spoiled my afternoon, with this here duck all covered with mud, all gone to pieces, struggling and gargling, and looking half dead. That looked pathetic. I felt right sick in my guts. So, I broke myself off a stick out of the hedge up the bank and waded out into the river. I beat on the water and the swan let go, so that the duck with a quack and a sneeze slobbered along away from the swan, and got away, flapping and shaking that's head down the stream.

Only now I got stuck myself: I had gone over to the side where the black mud was, and the mud at the bottom was about two or three feet deep. That was well over my rubber boots and they were full of water. I was in such a tizzy! I had walked right into it, and so there was me up to my thighs in water, with my boots caught in the mud so that wouldn't come out. That old swan was still angry and all fluffed up but luckily I had kept hold of my bit of stick and I sometimes used it to get my balance, and sometimes to beat on the water to scare off the swan. But when I couldn't get myself out of the deep mud I began to holler.

And who should come along but my Uncle Tom.

'Good God!' I heard him say. 'What's that bloody boy up to now?'

It was at that moment, just as he appeared, with his cap and his curled-up black-waxed whiskers, that I saw a large dead trout lying against the bank, a little way down. Nothing to do with me, but who'd believe that?

'That's all right, Uncle Tom,' I said. 'I was just scaring off a swan what was throttling a duck.'

'That's a funny good hummer,' my Uncle said. 'I wonder what he's really up to? All that popple and snaffle?'

'That's true,' I said.

'You'll be askin' me soon whether I want a ride on a dickey,' he said, staring around.

That's what they say in Norfolk: 'Have your father got a dickey, bor?' And then you answer 'Ah, and he want a fule to ride him.' My old Uncle thought I was taking him in something cruel. Anyhow, he had a good look round and he didn't see nothin': he stood there still a bit puzzled. All this time I was trying to get my boots out of the mud. That was all socky. At last, he held down the end of his stick, so that I could hold on to that. I pulled and at last I managed to get one boot out, and then the other. They came out with a great sucking noise.

'Thank you, Uncle Tom,' I said.

'You better hop off home quick boy and change your things. You sat down in that sluss a bit and I reckon you must be wholly wetshed.'

He seemed kindly after the rage he was in the day before. I didn't say nothin'.

'I found that old pheasant,' he said. 'Why didn't you tell me that'd been run over?'

'How d'you know?' I stuttered.

'Why, that was all crushed down one side,' he said. I couldn't think how you'd catched him bare handed.'

'He was still alive when I got him,' I said.

'Ah,' said Tom. 'And you finished him off masterful. Only … that in't a thing to get interested in boy, especially not out o' season.'

He twisted his whiskers at me, in a warning kind of way. Well, that was better. I thought we might get a bit more friendly now and I was just goin' to slarver a bit more to him when his bright old brown eye caught sight o' that fish.

Well, I didn't need no telling. I was gone before he could lift up his stick. Only I didn't go home to the farm. I ran up into Bayfield Woods to see if I could see my old Great Granny. At least she didn't know nothing bad about me.

THIRTEEN

Up in Bayfield Woods, my old Mum and Dad told me, live your old Great Granny. You ought to go and see her. She's ninety-two. She's got a well, ninety feet deep. Who do you think I am, I said, Little Red Riding Hood? This was meant to be a joke, but my old Mum didn't like me being sharp like that, nor did my Dad. They knew they ought to go and see Granny Bayfield more often, and they were guilty about that. Anyway, I promised to go up there. The trouble is that people like your old Mum and Dad, they have feelings about old Granny Bayfield, they think she's a dear, quaint old thing; only they never go and see her, or do nothing for her, shopping or nothing. Or perhaps they take her a cake once a year. But they think you ought to have the right sort of feelings about this trembly old person and you don't. Or, you don't yet. You don't have no reason to go and see them, until some kind of curiosity get hold of you. Well, since I was up here at Glandford I was curious. And now I was tankerous with every one else, I thought I might as well break new ground.

I walked up towards Glandford and then turned down the drive that went up to Bayfield Hall, past the lake, and on up into the woods. There were some big old trees up there and shrubs, fern, and bushes: it was dark in some parts of the wood. I reckon that was a real forest.

Great Grandmother's cottage was right up in the thickest part, with a little clearing and a well-cover. The cottage was built of brick and flint with slate tiles, with just a little garden full of lettuce, and beans. That was all quiet and there was a strong smell of dead leaves, a wood scent. It was just like being inside a big hall or cathedral. People said that was the smell of leaves that made people live so long up there. Do you know all round there people live to a remarkable age, old Cave told us! Granny Bayfield lived there with this woman companion, a relative, who'd given up her life to look after the old lady. Old Granny was such a clean and neat old lady, in a brown wool frock trimmed with lace. She stared at me with pale blue eyes, all watery. And then she kissed me. That was a real rum un. I don't mean any direspect when I say that was like being kissed by one of them old mummies in the Castle Museum. Her mouth was all shrivelled up, like an apple in store gone withered, though still sweet really. There were lines all round her mouth, and her face was as thin as greaseproof paper, but all yellow and cracked. Her face was all cracked with lines, like the ground in my old Dad's allotment, when there's a drought. Or then I thought it was like the neck of Timmy, my tortoise, before he froze to death last winter. The cracks ran this way and that way, and underneath all the network of lines there were tiny blue veins. You felt you could see through her nearly. But her hair was still dark, drawn back straight on each side of her head and she wore a little mob cap. So that all made a funny little old shaky head, like the head on a very old doll.

She put a little hand on my arm. Her hands were ever so small and you could see all the bones in them, and the veins and tubes that work the fingers. I took her hand and held it for a bit, but then I got frightened in case I broke that off, so I carefully put it back. Aunt Sarah always stood in the background and managed her a little bit. She looked a nice, tidy, plump woman, very quiet and kind, in a grey dress and boots with buttons, and hooks.

'So, you're Ken's boy,' Granny said. Her voice was all cracked like her face, all gravelly. 'Bless my heart alive,' she said in her Norfolk voice, 'I'm glad to see you, child, that I am.'

She was the oldest person I have ever seen in my life. I'm getting beyond the stage of believing in fairy stories: but I had a rum feeling up in those woods she'd turn me into something, or eat me, you know.

On her part, she knew nothing about youngsters and seemed to think the first thing you do with a boy is feed him with something. Well, I didn't mind too much.

'Have we any of Anna's loaf left, Sarah?'

'That we have.'

'Do you give him a nice slice with some honey on it. Do you like honey, boy? We have a hive up here, you know: they work for us. I don't know his name yet,' she added in a trembly way.

Now I have got to tell you, my first feeling with this wobbly old lady was that she might die any moment. I know that don't sound very kind. But she looked so frail I felt that if that wind blowed too hard or if I dropped something or the door slammed, she'd just drop down and become nothin' but a heap of dust and a little old bit of crumpled cloth. So I was very careful what I did, though I was determined to see down her well before I left because my old Dad said that was ever so deep. So, when old Sarah asked me if I'd like a drink, I said I'd like a glass of water.

'Don't you like milk?'

'No, thanks,' I said. 'I'd rather have a glass of water.'

They could see by the way I kept lookin' what I wanted.

'We're neither of us strong, we old ladies,' said Sarah. 'Do you think you could draw us a bucket from the well?'

"Course I will,' I said. 'I've heard about your well.'

'Ah,' said my old Great Granny. 'Do you be careful and all. We dread that well, if the truth be told. Mind you, that's safe enough, do you respect it.'

'That's very deep, my boy,' said the other woman. 'Some on 'em say that's the deepest well in the whole of Norfolk.'

She came with me and opened the cover. There was a winder built of stout posts, with a handle sticking out from the end. The whole thing was boxed in and painted brown. You opened a lid and there was the round brick well, falling away out of sight.

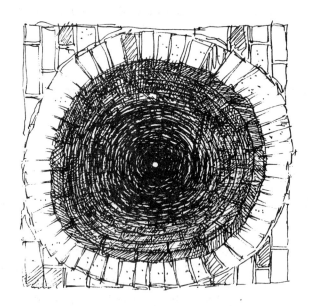

Looking down Granny Bayfield's well

As she opened the lid, a small pebble which had been lying on the cover fell and clanked against the cylinder. Then that fell into the well. As I put my head over, I didn't know what to look for and it was dark, so my eyes weren't adjusted. At last, I saw a tiny silver circle, about as big as a shilling, and just at that moment the pebble struck the surface, ages after that had dropped. An echoing little sound came whisperin' up the wall, like a musical sound from far away.

Down went the bucket clipped to a thin chain, down and down, and I unwound the handle. It seemed as if that would never reach the water. There was more of that funny musical noise, a queer sort of hollow echoing noise, as that swung against the side; and then a distant tinkling splash as it smacked against the water. Miles away, that clanked and tinkled, and sank. Now I turned the handle the other way.

'Slowly now, boy,' said Sarah, 'otherwise there'll be nothing in it by the time you get that to the top.'

So, ever so slowly, I wound up that heavy bucket, while that swung on the long chain. Every now and then the chain slipped into a groove, and a musical clank echoed down the long brick tube, vibrating and vibrating away. At last the wet chain came up, dripping, and then the bucket. The drips echoed too, down and down, and then up and up from the water far below.

That was sweet, cold water.

You'd never think that was likely, but any road I sat and talked to them old ladies all the rest of the afternoon, and had a cup of tea. But then old Granny Bayfield she got a bit tired and said while she was fair to middlin' in the morning, she was gettin' a bit more middlin' now that was late afternoon, so I better go off home. So I did.

I walked down through the woods in a rum old mood. That old woman she was so old! When she looked in my face, that was like the Almighty staring at you: her bright old eyes, in that shrivelled up little old face, seemed to go right through you. She was right out of the way of making mistakes or doing wrong: all she could do now was to go on living a bit, up in the quiet of them trees, and thinking about life. That was like visiting some rum old monk up in the mountains: so I came down out of the woods feeling as if I was sailing on air. I'd never met anyone over ninety. Only ten old grannies that age stretched end to end and you'd be back to the Normans; only three or four more, and you'd be back to the Anglo-

Saxons. I wondered what old Cave'd say when I told him that.

When I got down towards our road from Holt to Glandford, though, I heard people moving, and down on the side of the road I could hear someone talking. I recognised old Abbs from his humming and gasping, and then I saw old Charlie Bacon, dancing about, eating an apple. With them were the three Lightfoot boys, with a couple of sacks. These were full of apples, because I saw Tim Lightfoot pull one out and give it to old Abbs. He had a dressing strapped to his head with plaster. That made me feel a bit wobbly in my knees, so I kept well out of sight. I slipped from tree to tree, but I got near enough to hear what they were saying.

'First shugs!' old Abbs shouted, laughing. They both had an apple and bit that.

'You picked 'em too early, you soft buggers,' said old Charlie. 'They aren't maller.'

'They hain't got no … hum … foison in 'em yet,' said old Abbs, mongeing away.

'You have to make hay while the sun shine,' said one of the Lightfoot boys.

'Ah, hum … an' I know what kind they are an' all,' said old Abbs.

'They're Gascoign's Scarlet and there's only one tree of that kind around here.'

'Well, what about it?' asked another voice. 'Didn't you never go scrumpin'?'

'Ah,' said Charlie, 'only you don't want to discomfrontle a good old woman like poor old Anna Ransome.'

'Wah!' jeered Tim Lightfoot. 'She ha' got plenty. Have another one, Charlie. Might as well eat 'em now we got 'em.'

Charlie Bacon took another apple. 'They taste better when they're nicked,' he said, with his funny old giggle, rather childish. 'Hah! Hah!'

They were all sitting around on the side of the road. I was seeing all this through the eyes of my ninety-year-old Granny Bayfield because she was so old and out of this world. I felt myself a long way from these farm-workers after seeing her, and I didn't want to fall into their way of behaving no more, because I had got a different feeling from the simple way of life of them two old women up in the wood. Their poor, thin, worn hands, all worn out from collecting up sticks, and winding up water from the well! Would they

66

take stolen apples, or game that had been poached, like old Abbs and Bacon would? Of course not. There was something disrespectful about it.

I could hear Aunt Sarah's voice, what she'd say. 'Where did them apples come from, Tim Lightfoot?' If they'd been nicked, she'd never touch one. But old Abbs and Charlie were eating them, and talking to the Lightfoot boys as if they were their best chums. There was this feeling, I could see, among the men, the farm-labourer men in the village. They'd been good to me; but they also belong to Letheringsett village. And they were mumpers when that came to making anything useful that was lying around.

'Cor blast,' said Bob Lightfoot, the big one, 'my old man was mortally riled when Tim come home with his head broke.'

'Where's that little bugger this mornin'?' asked the older boy, Roger.

'He's ... hum ... got the day off,' said old Abbs. 'Do he have disobliged himself ... he's only a younker. Any old road, like I told your old man, anyone who start on him'll have me to deal with.'

I notched up old Abbs for that.

'We were a-goin' to ding some o' these apples at him, if he'd a bin in the field with you.'

'Ah,' was all old Abbs would say.

'Go you on home, wastin' stuff like that. I don't hold with it,' said Charlie.

'What, are you gettin' tankerous, too, old Charlie Bacon?' Tim said in a cheeky voice.

'Don't you give me that sort o' chelp,' said the old man, 'else you'll get a larrupin' ... phewt!' he spat. 'Them apples are like goose-gogs. They don't fare to be ready till nearly October, yew sorft little buggers!'

The boys went off, dragging their sacks. But Charlie and Abbs had been friendly enough with my enemies, and made me feel I was right not to take them in trust. I could never tell them about my find in the bank. That would be all round the village next day – after they'd filled their pockets. The way they went on talking made me sure I was right, however much they'd defended me, to stick to old Tom, and try to get in touch with old Cave.

'Ah ... tha's always the same, if people make off with things like that ... um ...' said old Abbs, wheezing reflectively. 'Tha's a mortal waste.'

'Remember that old deer last harvest?' said Charlie.

They were going to have a good old jaw now.

I knew from what Mr Walker said at breakfast that they were taking a couple of sacks of oats to a farm at Blakeney, to grind. Old Isaac had an oil engine and a grinder, but the belt had broke, and so he had sent his labourers to grind it at the farm of a friend of his. However, when they got just to the rise about Glandford, these two men had stopped for a bit of sun and a smoke, and a jaw. That has a nice spot by the woods, with warm silky grass to sit on, and there they'd be for a bit, clacking away.

'Old Lumpo, he found this here roebuck caught in some barbed wire and he killed that. Old Lightfoot helped him cut that up and they buried all the guts, and insides. Well, they brought all the joints up the Dog in the back o' old Lumpo's car under the seat – and could they sell that?'

'That was lovely meat an' all.'

'How do you know?'

'He sold me a bloody great haunch of it for a shillin'.'

'That he didn't!'

'I ate the lot an' all.'

'I reckon you must 'a bin the only one. Old Johnny, he said, "Why, this here meat look like a casualty." "Blast," they said. "Do you shut up – old Tom Ransome's in the other bar."'

'That'd 'a bin a bad case, poachin' a deer.'

'Well, in the ind he give that away. And, do you know, everybody buried their pieces!'

'No!'

'That they did. Their old missuses, they got the wind up. Old Ma Johnson and young Mrs Biddle – they daren't cook that, in case they were caught doin' it, and they got their old men to dig a hole at night, and bury the bugger!'

'Hum ... oogh ... Well, I had a chop or two off on it as well as you.'

'Ah, well,' said Charlie with a sigh. 'Everythin' have an ind and a puddin' ha' got two ...'

They got up and got the old tractor going. Abbs drove and Charlie stood holding the two sacks of oats against the end of the trailer.

'Hallo together,' the old man shouted at two girls who were bicycling the other way. 'Come you on for a trip to Blakeney Fair?'

68

But they took no notice.

'That old man is a-mawkin',' said one, as they rode past me.

'Old muck spout,' said the other. 'Time he was pushing up the dead nettles.'

They laughed as they pedalled on. I walked thoughtfully back to the farm. That was a warm August afternoon, with the air smelling faintly of dust from the crops being harvested everywhere. In the trees the wood pigeons called ceaselessly: 'Take two cows, taffy, take two cows, take!' Who could I trust? I thought mostly about my Granny, up in the wood where the ground was all covered with deep springy leaf-mould. I had a phrase in my head that I'd heard old Isaac say, when I'd said I'd like to go and see my Granny.

'Ah, boy,' he'd said, 'she's very, very old.' With a sigh, 'A ground sweat cure all disorders.'

After thinkin' a bit I understood what he said.

I watched them old Lightfoot boys going down the road and had a bit of a think about them, too. I was afraid of them, I dare say, in case they set on me. But I didn't hold nothing against 'em. I just thought they were half-rocked, to come up and ding me like that, without any reason.

They swung their shoulders and were a-mongeing them half-ripe apples, hulling the cores over the hedge. They saw an old hen pheasant with her chicks running along the side of the hedge like they do. She was teaching them to peck at the greenfly and that, I reckon. Any old how, Tim, he broke off a stick and larraped at her, makin' them all fall over and run, and then tried to kill her chicks with stones and sods of earth as they scuttled under some blackberry brambles. Then they got tired of that and just started pulling sticks of hawthorn down out of the hedge, breaking them, and leaving them like that. All I knew was, if I'd 'a done any of them things, Uncle Tom would have come out of somewhere and caught me at it. No one never caught them. As I watched them, a cloud come over and the light went a bit dull, and them boys seemed to merge into the earth. They had these here dark clothes on, dark greys and browns, and grey shirts. I reckoned they were earth people. They'd always be nicking turnips and apples, tormenting old frogs and badgers, and killing rabbits and game: then they'd disappear into the landscape. Old Charlie and Albert were like that, too, really. I was a city boy, do you know?

They didn't like me nor did they like my Uncle Tom. Now

they had robbed my uncle, out of spite. Their spite against me wasn't only because I was a foreigner, that was because of something else, and that weren't either because Tom was a game warden. It was because of the Shell Museum and all that stood for. That was because we looked further than our noses and had a thought or two, like old Cave had got into my mind, or like Sir Alfred had put into Tom's: we had ideas. I know what they'd say, though, like they say about gardeners up here: 'A line and a rule guide many a fule.'

I sighed now as I wandered down along the road, in the same direction as those Lightfoot boys, who had gone far out of sight. I was badly cut off from my old Uncle Tom now, but when I first come down to North Norfolk we were ever so close. And the closest we'd been was when he was showing me his Shell Museum.

FOURTEEN

Well, we were well ahead with the harvest, despite the storm, so we slacked off a bit. That was clear next morning; we'd get the last barley into that stack that day. There was a nice warm breeze that kept rustling the trees about, and there were some low little clouds kept driving over, so that was nice and cool to work. The trees were going a bit yellow here and there now, and there was a little touch of autumn in the air. As we came up to dinner time there was about two good loads left for the afternoon. So, there was a kind of end-of-harvest air about old Abbs and Charlie Bacon.

'I'm sick of that old beer,' said Charlie. 'Why don't we git some cider for a change?'

'Where'd you get cider round here?' asked old Abbs.

'Tha's nearer 'n you think!'

'I've lived here all my life and I never come across no cider ...'

'There's a little old press over at Honey.'

'Go you on! Ogh!'

But there was. Old Abbs was so much a Letheringsett village man he didn't even know the world the other side of the Cromer–Kings Lynn main road. We all got on the blue Ford tractor, old Abbs driving and me and Charlie sitting up on the mudguards, and drove to Thornage.

'If anyone ask you, boy, the eujackapivvy on the trailer's broke, and we're going to get a new pin for it from the blacksmith in Thornage.'

But we weren't: we were just going there with our stone jar to get a gallon of cider. As we passed the flint farmhouse old Charlie laughed.

'There she is, old Mrs Walker.' He mimicked her. '"I saw them men going down on the tractor, Isaac: what are they a-doin' joy-riding about on your paraffin? They oughtn't t'imitate to go ridin' about on your tractors, scalifizin' about like dizzy fules."'

To me old Abbs said, 'She wouldn't like you going up the high road lookin' so shucky! She'll be quizzin' you boy: you tell her we broke our snafflin' shackle.'

'What's that?' I said.

'Ah, what is it, I wonder? ... Only that's what you want to tell her!'

He winked hard at me. I began to think I was in a rum old position, because I had to do everything they told me, and yet here they were doing something their employer wouldn't approve of – and they were expecting me to tell hummers about it. Well, I would see how that worked out. But that made me wonder what kind of men they were really like, and how they'd behave if I was caught doing something wrong again. However, I couldn't help getting into the spirit of it as the old tractor bounced along on its big wheels along the asphalt road and over the Cromer Road, and down the side-roads to Hunworth.

In a little old building, in bad repair, there was this very old cider press, overgrown with ivy and elder, with little or no glass in the windows, and full of things lying about higgledy-piggledy, shovels and wooden sieves, and bottles. There were several barrels piled up at one end on top of one another, and long-handled wooden scoops and baskets everywhere. That wasn't, of course, quite apple-time yet, but one farmer had sent in a barrel of windfalls and some Beauty of Bath, and these were being put into the press. There was this lovely smell of rotten, ripe apples, and the sludgey noises as one of the workmen churned up the windfalls with a bright clean shovel. Then the box of chopped apples was turned into the body of the press, a huge wooden box, with a screw over it and a beam, folds of zigzag cloth of some kind, with a metal spout for the juice to run out.

There was a lot of chaff as the barrel of apples was shovelled by degrees into the press.

'Why, Charlie, you don't want to get on to this here stuff at your age, boy. You're bad enough as it is.'

'Do you know old Abbs didn't know this here press was here?'

'We only work in the autumn when the farmers send their apples,' one of the men said to me. 'Rest of the time tha's all locked up. The cider's all kept for a year, in the barrel, o' course, to ferment.'

The men began to turn the screws and the top of the press squelched down. Bubbles and froth came up through the cracks. It all looked such a ramshackled business, everything screwed to-gether with old bolts, and the press plugged here and there with big sacks, and spider webs and leaves and stalks were over everything.

72

But the juice which came out into the gleaming buckets was clear and sparkling. One of the men put a little hand shovel under the flow of the apple juice and handed it to me.

'Try that, boy,' he said, laughing.

'Will that make me drunk?' I said.

'Not yet, boy, not till tha's worked, that 'un't.'

I balanced the shovel up to my face and gingerly put its shining blade with its curved up edges to my lips. A stream of apple juice shot into my mouth, sweet and delicious. It was full of air and very dry, and refreshing. Some went down my shirt.

I liked it better than the cider, which seemed not to taste so appley. That was dry to the taste and seemed harmless, just like nice water with a fruity flavour. I suppose I drank half a pint at the cider press and then we seemed to be back in the field, though it was really six miles and half an hour later. There I drank another half pint with my bread and cheese, when we got back under the trees.

We didn't sleep that day, because we'd had our outing, and Charlie and old Abbs wanted now to get the job done. So, we put our stuff away and tucked the bottle under the hedge to keep cool, and they started off with their pitchforks. I say they, because I couldn't walk. I seemed to have flown back from Hunworth on the tractor mudguard. Old Abbs was driving fast, and they had done quite a lot of giggling and gasping. I could remember that.

'Stop gimblin', blast, you old sawney!' old Abbs cried.

I could remember Charlie laughing and holding on. But I noticed a kind of light, floating feeling in my legs and body; I had put that down to the tractor bouncing, and rolling about.

But when we got there I just couldn't walk at all. When I got off I just fell down. Then I got hold of my pitchfork and pushed that into the ground, and gradually heaved myself to my feet. Was I paralysed? Had I got some horrible illness? Perhaps I'd had a stroke like old Aunt Marjorie at Briston? I was frightened at first, but then I realised that was the cider. I wasn't drunk. The field wasn't going round, my speech wasn't slurred and my head was reasonably clear. That was just that: I couldn't do anything with my legs. They just wouldn't work. They were paralysed. That was no good getting to my feet, so I let myself go and simply lay there for an hour. In the distance I could hear old Charlie and Abbs giggling about it.

'Blast, I thought we'd lost you boy. That's that old cider: you want to watch that old stuff!'

73

That's all everybody said: but I couldn't see the gimblin' stage had worked off for them, they were still a bit clumsy with the forks. And old Abbs had scratched his legs with his, down by his shin, and that was all covered with splashes of dried blood.

Anyhow, that took us till about six before we got the last wobbly load up on to the stack. Charlie was grumbling at old Abbs now.

'Take that bor quietly,' he shouted. 'Don't come round so sharp, or that'll go down and we'll be here pickin' that up all again in the bloody dark.'

'Wah, hold your slaverin' jaw!' shouted old Abbs. They were gettin' really ugly now.

At seven o'clock there was still half a load, and they sent me off.

'Old Charlie'll stay with me to finish this off: you better go home quick 'cause old Isaac have his tea at ha' past six as you know.'

So, to be quicker, I set off across the cleared stubble field: I thought I'd walk through between the wood and the hedge, and come on to the road by the track. Well, for some reason, perhaps because the cider was still in my head, I went through the wood, following a sort of clearing, and came out on the Smoker's Hole side. Then I made my way down the wide of the wood.

Suddenly I heard a sort of jumping and crashing noise, and stopped still. I stopped and kept quite still: and the noise stopped. But then suddenly my legs gave way a bit – that was the effect of the cider still – and I quickly righted myself. At the noise of this, the noises started again, and there was a frightened squeal, a high-pitched squeal of fear and pain, like you hear from rabbits in the harvest field. I crept towards the noise on all fours, quietly, and saw that was a hare. How it happened, I couldn't tell, but some snares had been put over some rabbit warrens in the banks along the side of the wood, and this hare had caught its foot in the noose. Its leg was all stripped of fur and bloody, worn down almost to the bone. It looked horrible and I felt a bit sick. I reckon that was partly the cider hangover. Any old how, I felt a chill of pain and fear go down my inside. What was I to do? I didn't want to kill the hare: that looked too big and beautiful like a big cat. That was all bright brown with a white undercoat, and its head was lifted high with its tall ears up, its eyes big and full of dark fear, its sides heaving quickly. I was afraid it would ruin its leg by kicking and pulling, if I shot forward.

At first I tried creeping towards it, trying to calm it by making sucking noises with my lips, but this was no good. That simply backed and bucked, and tried to wrench itself away. So, I simply grabbed it and held my hands round its neck, and nipped its back part in my thighs. Suddenly, never mind the cider, all my strength came back to me: I more or less sat on the poor thing, determined that shouldn't destroy itself in mad pain, and frenzy. At last, I managed to nip the squealing old leveret between my legs so tight that I could free my hands. I hoped that wouldn't bite me. I held one of its thighs, the one of the wounded hind leg, hard with one hand, and worked and worked at the wire noose with the other. It was tight, blood-smeared and caught in the fur. But it also had a twig caught in it, so at last I managed to get a finger in, and worked that open. That seemed ages, and I was sweating and grunting. The hare every now and then made a frantic heave, and when I clung tighter, it squealed its high note. At last I got its paw free of the snare and could see that although it was skinned a bit, it wasn't wounded: once it was free he gave me a good old scrape with his claws, and made my hand bleed. But at least that leg was good.

I was just seeing it was good when I heard a shout.

'Leave them bloody snares alone, boy!' It was Charlie.

'Why, he've got a hare or something,' old Abbs was wheezing. 'Ogh … phum!'

But above on the hill by the wood I saw my Uncle Tom. I let my hare go and that went across the stubble at about sixty miles an hour. I went off behind him at about twenty, my legs feeling like water again. They could all think what they liked. But this was the third time my Uncle Tom had seen me, looking as if I was poaching. I had all the bad luck. I didn't care about Charlie and old Abbs: I could think of some hummer to tell them, and if the snares were theirs, why were they were robbing their employer on the quiet, anyway? Only, didn't I have all the luck?

FIFTEEN

I was glad to get out of everybody's way as early as I could, when the morning came all grey, and soggy, with sheets and sheets of rain. Donald was in a proper old gloom when I came down, cursing and muttering in the dark corners of the kitchen, looking for his highlows.

'D'you want to see what tha's really like?' he grumbled at me.

'What what's like?' I asked.

'Bloody old farmin',' he said. 'Sod it! I ha' got to do them old sheep – I mustn't leave 'em any longer. Why, they're bein' eaten alive.'

'What by?' I said. 'Dogs?'

'No, blast, boy,' said Donald. 'Ma-aggots.' He held up his little finger and wiggled it at me, to show me how a maggot grub wiggle.

I didn't feel like my breakfast after that.

Any old how, I wasn't going to let him see I was too pamplin' to see to any datty old farm job, so I said I'd come. And I was glad to get out of the road, as I said.

The rain had stopped now and that was nice, and fresh. Donald wore a cap and an old fawn raincoat all covered with oil spots. We stomped along in our rubber boots on the wet road. I had a long stick and Donald had a painter's pot of hot tar, and a short tar brush. We were going to have to whop the sheep into a corner of the field, pen them in with a roll of netting, then take them one by one to look at and if there were any maggots in them we'd have to get them out, and paint the places with tar. I made a note to tell my old Mum if she get a shoulder of lamb that smell a bit tarry, she'd better throw it away, not start roasting that.

'Wer!' said Donald. 'They're the wrong sort o' sheep, tha's what it is. Old Isaac keep them down by the river in that water meddie and tha's too wet for 'em. Sheep like to be up on the dry. They get real claggy down there in all that mud.'

So he went on grumbling and grousing, all the way to the water meadow. Then we started whoppin' up into a corner. By this time I'd done a lot of cow whopping: that was a real sport even on the outskirts of Norwich City, like where we live out at Mile Cross.

Farmers used to drive their old bullocks and that in herds through the city to the cattle market, runnin' into gates, and dropping their plops all along the road. We used to get to know when the market days were and on holidays we used to get ready for it.

'Are you goin' a cow whoppin', bor?' everyone would shout. And when the cattle appeared all the little old boys would run to the hedges and break theirselves off a long stick. As he came in from his outlying village early in the morning the stockman might have only one boy helping him, but as he drove through the outskirts he'd gather a whole band of old boys, all brandishing sticks and jumping about to keep the cattle going the right way.

They didn't expect nothing for it. That was done just for the excitement. You'd see some little old boy only about two feet high going down the side-roads and holding up his hand to stop the buses and lorries: the traffic'd stop for him because he had his cow-whoppin' stick in his hands, and his legs and boots all covered in cow muck. Then the old bullocks would come along and start trying to nose their way off sideways (for although we called that cow-whoppin' that was really bullock whoppin') and then the little old boy'd give them such a thwacking on their hind quarters they'd soon gambol back into line. Mind you, you shouldn't whack 'em too hard, else they'd start and stampede and go through somebody's shop window, and that might bruise the meat. So, the old boys had to keep nipping ahead, and judging their whoppin' so that was just right. And, of course, now and then, one of them beasts would turn nasty, specially one of the bullocks that hadn't been properly castrated, and he'd put his head down, and go for you. One went for me once and then he changed his mind, only the road was slippery with cow muck, and he started to slide. There was me with a quarter of a ton of beef sliding towards me and I only just managed to duck under a railing at a bus stop. Lord! He hit that railing, thuck! I reckon if I'd been the other side I'd have been cold meat myself rather than him, for that's what he was going to be next day. That didn't seem to have no effect on him: he only snuffed hard and tossed his head and heels, and off he went. You had to look out for some of the ones with horns, though: they'd give you a datty old look if you waved your cow-whoppin' stick at them.

Well, tha's cow whoppin', and sometimes you'd get carried away and find yourself right up in the City, right out on Castle Meadow, driving 'em up on the cobbles among the pens, everyone shouting 'Who-up!' and 'High-up!' and thousands of beasts baa-ing and moo-ing, and everything pushing and shoving and what my old Grandfather William used to call 'show kite' everywhere, with a strong smell of cow piddle and beer, and the auctioneers shouting 'Seven-five, seven-five, seven-ten, seven-ten, eight anywhere, eight, eight-five, eight-ten I'm bid. Nine anywhere? Yes nine ...' and so on. That was lively and I never minded walking home, even though I was only ten or eleven, because cow hairs were sticking to my stick, and my rubber boots were all muck an' straw.

Donald and I had a rough old time with those claggy old sheep of Issac Walker's, though. They were the most awkward old buggers I'd ever met in the animal world. Now I reckon you think sheep are silly and dim: they aren't a bit. They're cunnin' old devils, yet they're panicky. I've seen them break into an old lady's garden and settle down mangeing her wallflowers and that, but if the old farmer come along and say 'Cup!' they'll wag their old thick, woolly tails, and they'll follow one another through the gap just where they come in; they knew they were doin' wrong. But if she come out in her nightie and start a duller at 'em, they'll go off everywhere, humping sideways at the hedge, trampling over her old cabbage plants, getting their heads stuck in her runner-bean poles like a lot of clowns. They only do that to annoy.

Well, these datty, grey, old sheep of old Isaac's were like that. They'd all huddle in the wrong corner, and when we tried to urge them along they'd slip past us and all spread out all over the field, some of 'em coughing as if we were running them to death, and baa-ing like they were dying of shock. Donald was cussing them and whenever he got near one he'd kick it. Anyhow, after a while we learnt how to do it. You have to spread out and only move a little bit, then stop. Gradually, step by step, you urge them to go down where you want them; if one thinks he's going to sneak out, just stretch out your hand and he'll turn back. Only this time we had the roll of wire netting unrolled and at last we had them all penned in a corner, plumes of steam coming out of them, and them all trembling and baa-ing as if they were going to be pole-axed. We were all of a muckwash, and fit to drop.

'Now you old bastards,' said Donald.

We made a kind of narrow corridor and Donald hauled one old sheep along it so we could get at him. Funny thing was they were docile when you get one alone by itself, and old Donald, instead of kicking it or swearing at it, got all motherly. I had to hold the sheep by its head while he dug down into its datty, old, grey woollen coat, parting it right down to the white wool and then the skin. He kept sniffing 'em too: they smelt all tallow and sheepmuck as it was, but he was smelling for bad meat, rot in the flesh.

When he found it, that looked horrible, dark and nasty; then he would press with his thumbs, and out would slide these big white maggots. That made me feel dizzy, to think that these poor animals had maggots living in their flesh, crawling about under the skin. Donald grunted and puffed, and when he pressed the old sheep would quiver and try to bolt, so we had to grip harder, and hold on. They've got some strength in their hind quarters, I can tell you!

'Tha's all account of old Isaac not dippin' 'em properly,' said Donald. 'Flies lay their eggs in the wool coat, then you ha' got t' dip 'em, to kill the eggs. He's a bit mean with the dip, so tha's what happen. Them old maggots, when they hatch out they dig into the bodeh.'

Then, when he'd got all the maggots squeezed out, he'd put on a dab of the tar with his brush. He'd work that well in and the old sheep would jump, because that'd sting. Stockholm tar that was called.

'Whup! You old bugger,' he'd sing out, grabbing that hard by the wool. 'Cup here!'

After a while that got interesting, and I had a go. While Donald did the main bits up behind the neck on the back of the sheep, I went over their flanks. Donald held on to an ear and I got hold of the old sheep's tail: that was a mucky job. I squeezed those maggots out myself: you had to press out a bit from the place where the skin was broken and out they'd slide. That was satisfying making 'em ooze out. You had to poke and poke to get every single one out. That was a foosey old job.

'You don't want to leave one in,' said Donald, 'else that'll goo right putrid in a couple o' weeks.'

There was one sheep where his whole shoulder had gone bad, with his wool dropping off, all blue and green underneath, swarming.

'He'll have to goo,' said Donald, makin' a sign with his finger under his throat.

So we were saving them old sheep from being eaten alive. All day we were squeezing out these maggots, and daubing on this tar.

79

But the old sheep were so datty, with mud caked on their coats. Their feet didn't look too good, either, Donald said: a bit rotty. After a while that got warm and drew out the smell even more, and there were all sorts of old flies coming after them and us – we had to keep waving them away, but they bit at our eyes and stung, and kept comin' back and back to our hands. They walked boldly right up into your nostril, so when you drew in a breath you nearly sucked a big fly up your nose. These old flies were getting datty with the rotten bits of the sheep and then walking into our eyes.

I hated that. I liked cleaning the poor old sheep up, but I got all messed up about what to believe about it. I mean, why did God make flies, to put their eggs in the coats of sheep, to eat them alive when they hatched out? How was it that an animal could get other living things in his flesh, mongeing off him as he walked about? I put that to Donald.

'Well, there you are,' he said. 'Tha's how it is – one thing live at th' expense of another. You watch them old thrushes, boy, pullin' up them old worms all day. That en't nice for them old worms, is it? They're eaten alive, en't they? You like a nice mussel, dorn't you, or a nice bit o' roast lamb?' He laughed, showing his teeth, a bit like Isaac.

'But right inside the sheep,' I said, watching the one that had been condemned, lumping about with his wormy shoulder all green and greasy under the rotten wool. 'If old Isaac hadn't dipped them at all, they'd all be rotten.'

'Ah, that they would,' said Donald, deep in the coat of another sheep.

'What did they do in the old days?' I asked.

'Did what we did, I reckon,' said Donald. 'Squeezed the buggers out when they could. Washed and dipped how they could. Tha's a right old struggle all the time: flies in the bloody turnips; flies in the bloody apples; weevil in the bloody wheat. They don't say nawthin about that at the bloody old harvest festival.'

'What would the Reverend Toft say?' I wondered. My Aunt Anna was always on about what a marvellous man the Reverend Toft was.

'He keep his bloody mouth shut about things like that,' said Donald. 'If he ha' got any sense.'

'There ought to be a bit about it in the Bible if you looked,' I said.

'Ah, there is,' said Donald, and all of a sudden he became a quite different person. His eyes lit up and he said '"In the sweat of your face shalt thou eat bread" – tha's what that say. And that say, "That shall bruise thy hand and thou shalt bruise his heel."'

'Do you mean,' I said, digging the tar brush into the empty maggot holes in a sheep's back, 'that these here troubles come because some people sin?'

'Ah!' said Donald. And then suddenly that all came out, as if somethin' was driving him.

'"By the great force of my disease is my garment changed ... My skin is black upon me, and my bones are burned with heat ... His flesh is consumed away, that it cannot be seen; and his bones that were not seen stick out ..."'

I stood there with my jaw dropped. Where did old Donald get all that from? His eyes were bright yellow now and he stood up with his pot of tar as if doing some business in church.

'"Who teacheth us more than the beasts of the field, and maketh us wiser than the fowls of heaven?"'

'Are you chapel or church?' I asked nervously.

'En't either!' declared Donald. 'Old Tofts he come along one day and he said how I ought to thank the Lord for all the stuff in my vegetable garden. "You ha' done a lot o' work," he said, "only the Lord hev done more." "Ah," I said, "only th' Almighty made a bloody mess on it when He had that all to himself." He didn't like that ... only I read a lot,' Donald added, and looked at me slyly. 'I don't need no bloody parson to tell me what that mean. I can read that in the backs of them old sheep and in old Isaac's winter barley while that grow.'

'Say some more,' I said.

He seized my coat with his tarry hands.

'"Has thou entered into the treasures of the snow? Or hast thou seen the treasures of the hail? ... By what is the light parted? ... Oh, ah ... What do that say? ... "To satisfy the desolate and the waste ground ... and to cause the bud of the tender harb to spring forth ..."'

'Where do that all come from?' I said. All these words seemed so strange and lovely, while we stood pressed into the woolly side of that last sheep, ready to dig his infection out. Donald picked up the tar pot again, and waved that about.

'"Who hath put wisdom in the inward parts? ... Who can stay the bottles of heaven?"'

81

There was a pause while Donald rattled his brush round the tar-pot, pickin' up the last of the disinfectant.

'Tha's the Book of Job, boy,' he said. There was water in his eye.

'What do that say?' I asked, my jaw rather hanging down, to find all this coming out of Donald.

'That say, why do the old sheep go maggoty? That say, why do blokes get pushes, and old mawthers get eaten up with cancer?'

'And why do they?' I asked.

'For reasons you on't never understand: 'cause tha's all there: that was put there, and you're in it. You have to take that or leave that – you can't do nawthin about it: "things too wonderful for me, which I knew not". Ah!'

Suddenly, old Donald lost his prophetic look. He dabbed the last place on that last sheep and we let him go hoppity away up the open field.

'Tha's a rum un, en't it?' asked Donald looking at me a bit sideways. He wasn't sure how I'd take the revelation of his Biblical knowledge. When he sat there gloomy at breakfast, or drove up and down the fields silently, all that poetry was running through his head. That was why he was so quiet always.

There was a rum kind of excitement about God and that, in some of them Norfolk people. I'd come across this with my old Granny Melton. She must have had a terrible life with old William and all his drinking, and all them children, in that little old house by the works. But I remember when I was about eight we all went with all the old family and her to chapel. That was made of corrugated iron-painted green, and there was a harmonium some old woman had to pump with her feet while she played it. There were dozens of them in there, all in black and Sunday best with hats on, and I was crushed in among all these women alongside my Granny. Well, you should have heard how they sung – Easter that was. You'd think they were praising the Lord for making 'em rich ladies with mansions and chicken dinners, and rose gardens all their lives, instead of poor working women on short commons. They sang about heaven above the sky and what I remember most was their 'hallelujahs':

> Christ the Lord is risen today!
> Ha-ha-a-a-le-luu-ja!

Our triumphant Holy Day!
Ha-ha-a-a-a-le-luu-ja!

They nearly took the tin roof off. I remember looking up at my old Granny's face, and that was all lit up like old Donald's when she sang that, and she gripped my hand, and the bits of lace and wax fruit on her black bonnet all shook with passion. She was going up there, that was evident. She didn't want to stay down here where the fly get in the sheep and where them old fire buckets hung at the end of her ugly little grey street, and where old William come home incapable. She was off with the Lord, as soon as she could.

I thought about her, warbling away in chapel, as I stood beside old Donald back at Home Farm, scrubbing that mixture of tar and tallow, maggot juice and blood off our hands. Donald hadn't said nothing more on the way home, nor did he say anything at the sink, nor at tea. Only he kept shooting me a funny old glance, as if he could have said a lot, if I'd asked for it.

I felt real Norfolk when I was with Donald.

SIXTEEN

Now I must tell you something really bad that happened. The harvest was over and they didn't need my help, so I could take time off and just muck about, so, next day, I set off up to the hedge where the warren was, where I had found that twisted article I believed was very old, and made of gold. I hadn't heard from old Cave and I reckoned he must be on holiday. I took a roundabout way through the woods, so if anyone saw me they wouldn't wonder why I was so interested in that particular hedge and that bit of old Isaac's field.

The rumours were flying about how I took after my father when he was a boy and how I was a right natural poacher. So, maybe some of them thought I was setting snares and hiding game, or something: you never know.

Well, this time when I got down and groped into the burrow opening I had worked – that thing had gone! I went all cold at that. Then I thought, don't be stupid: some old rabbit had been scratching about and that's got moved. But I dug around and dug around with my hand, and all I could find was loose soil. The torque just wasn't there!

I felt all the blood drain from my face, like happens when you get caught out doing something wrong. I began to wonder whether I'd ever seen the thing, and whether I hadn't been just romancing over a piece of old wire or something. But then I felt really awful, because I had told Cave: like as not he was getting ready to drive over to Letheringsett and, when he got here, what would he think? I knew he didn't think much of me, and schoolmasters are suspicious, anyway. He'd perhaps think I was playing some kind of trick on him. How was I going to convince him that I had really recognised an old piece of gold like those ones in the museum in London? I hadn't even done a drawing of it.

And I sat there on the side of the stubble field, with the butterflies fidgetting about in the hedge, and I began to wonder whether the thing had ever existed at all. Perhaps I had dreamt the whole thing?

And then – what did it matter? I gazed miserably at the hedge with the burrow holes undermining it, and the heaps of rabbit spoil in among the roots of the hawthorns and sloe. Some of the leaves were beginning to turn colour and the landscape was sleepy with the coming end of summer: the mists in the shadows were turning blue. The fields were stripped, and looked clean and empty, all done with the year

What did it matter whether or not some ornament someone had dropped was recovered or not? In old Isaac Walker's yard there was this heap of old bits of binder and that, rusting away with the nettles growing through it all – nobody bothered about that. That was yesterday. Who cared about yesterday?

No doubt that was one of the Lightfoot boys. I might have got really Norfolky down here, and I had become a bit of a country boy, but they were more cunning than I was: he had no doubt stalked me down here, and watched. What was it I was up to? Any old how, he had found it.

Now, what would he have done with it? As I thought, I started chucking stones off the stubble into the hedge and watched where they fell. I remembered the Lightfoot boys, with the apples, and the way they'd been larricking about in the lanes. And suddenly my other self began to take over, the thoughtful me, who had learned a bit at school with old Cave and them, and thought about death and time. Yes, I said to myself, that thing was there and it is important for us to study yesterday so we can know about ourselves, even if we do die.

Them old boys were thoughtless; we do need to think: under there was something we need to think about. I must find that torque before old Cave came up to North Norfolk. But where would I start looking? And then I had a premonition, as I threw another stone into the hedge. I was thinking of the Lightfoot's slinging those apples about. When they found the torque, they'd throw it. They'd not recognise it's value: they'd just see it as a thing a boy'd pick up, like a penknife or an old bottle. And when they got it, they'd just sling it away, not caring where it went.

I got a stick and marked out a big circle, from the burrow entrance, as far away as I thought a boy could throw a thing like that. I tested this using a stone. And then I set about walking up and down with my eyes on the ground, searching for it. In the end I reckon I must have got to know every stone on that patch. I found an old shoe and I found plenty of bits of binder twine. I was home late and old Mrs she gave me a going over about where I had been to, to be late for supper. But I didn't find the thing, and I lay awake for a long time into the night worrying about that.

SEVENTEEN

Since I had been at old Isaac Walker's my Uncle Tom seemed to have been pushed a long way from me, further away than my old Mum and Dad in Birmingham. Yet I always expected him now to pop up in the landscape, with the mole on his ruddy cheek and his cap, his waxed whiskers, and his watch-chain. Ah, and his stick, which he'd give a little twist to suddenly, if he caught sight of trouble.

He'd twitched that stick when he saw me pick up that dead pheasant. He'd twitched that stick after he'd held it out to me when he saw that big trout in the mud. And he'd twitched that stick when he'd seen me let the hare go. I was wholly on the wrong side of that stick. He must be convinced by now I was a bad 'un and if he saw me go back to that warren to dig, he'd be convinced. He'd be bound to see me.

Well, I felt I still must try, so one day I took another day off and I walked over to Glandford. But first I watched from a little way off to make sure Aunt Anna was alone and old Tom was out. Then I thought I'd really press my luck: I walked in.

'Why, Duffy, that is nice to see you,' she say smilin' and twinklin' her old eyes, with a big smile on her face, her little old apple cheeks shining. 'Would you like an apple?'

'Why, yes, Aunt Anna,' I say, trying to look as though I hadn't thought the first apples might be just about ready. She watched me closely as she said that.

'You better have a couple, my little man, seeing they're only little old Beauty of Bath ones,' she said, head down in the basket. 'They're nice and sweet though.'

I couldn't stand it really when she called me 'my little man' because she used to call me that when I was three or four, but I thought I'd work a bit on it, and be a bit childish, to get her sympathy.

'Can I have a look down your well?' I asked, polishin' the apples on my corduroy trousers.

'Well, do you be careful,' she said. But she wiped her hands on her apron and lifted the top. I held tight on to the brick wall surround and looked over. But that weren't half as deep as Granny Bayfield's. That made more of a singsong, though, when you touched the chain, because that had a bigger shaft down to the water.

'I tell you what,' she said. 'You can draw up a bucket for me, save me the trouble.'

So, with a thrill I clicked the bucket on the metal clasp and whizzed the handle round until the pail hit the water below.

'Steady with that handle, boy,' said the little old woman. 'Don't you let go o' that or we shall lose the lot.'

My idea had been to let the handle fly round by itself. But if you did that, she said, the chain might snap and you'd have no water until that was repaired. Anyway, that might give you a crack on the jaw. 'And your Uncle Tom would be wholly aggravated.'

'I see,' I said, biting my apple, as the pail sank. Then I wound it up gingerly, taking a look at her face now and then, and then lookin' back carefully at that bucket comin' up.

We put two full pails of bright clear well water in Aunt Anna's scullery. They scraped with a noise like tin bells on the clean, worn-brick floor. Eveything was always clean, primed and ready in Aunt Anna's house.

'Now we'll put that lid down and lock him up. You must never forget that or one day something terrible will happen.'

She paused, snicking the padlock. The tall poplars across in the hedge from her back door rustled and a blackbird sang loudly in the garden. She looked at me carefully with her bright, pale, blue eyes with their crowsfeet wrinkles in the corner. 'You're not a bad boy, are you?'

I looked down sideways a bit and then bit another bite out of my apple. I mumbled something.

'Parding?' she said.

'Don't think so,' I said, embarrassed.

'F'rinstance ...' she said, staring hard across at me, thoughtful. 'You wouldn't steal people's apples would you, Duffy?'

'Not ... not around here,' I said.

'What do you mean by that?' she said, rather sharp.

'Not while I'm on holiday up here,' I blushed. 'I bin in enough trouble up here already.'

'Ah,' she said, still listening.

'Boys do steal apples,' I said, thinking I might as well tell the truth. 'I might have a go at home – at Mile Cross if I got in with a crowd ... just one or two to eat, or a turnip out of a field.'

'But you wouldn't strip nearly a whole tree, before they was ripe, and take away a whole box, and throw down all the ones you couldn't be bothered with, would you now?'

'Not me,' I said, and that wasn't a hummer either. I hate that sort of thing.

'Now do you come and see,' she said, walking vigorously up the garden, through my Uncle Tom's neat green rows of tall brussel sprouts, big fat onions with tops drying off, his runner beans all writhing over one another with loads of red blossoms and big long beans hanging down, up to the back of the garden. There was a big tree. I had seen that covered with fruit a few weeks ago. Big, red, shiny fruit, Gascoign's Scarlet, she said they were. Now they were nearly all gone. I could see that and I knew where they'd gone.

'I remember all that fruit,' I said. 'They were big, red ones. Oh, there's one,' I said, pointing to one left on the tree.

Her eyes were full of tears.

'They're all gone,' she said, bending down to a gap in the hedge. 'They all went out here and, look, they've chucked them about anywhere.'

The field beyond was full of half-chewed, broken and crushed apples, lying in the mud in the bottom of the hedge.

'And that kind aren't properly ready until near October.'

'That's wicked,' I said. 'I bet my Uncle Tom was cross.'

She looked me hard in the face.

'He don't show it ...' she said. 'But he were wholly cross. He hate anyone abusin' his garding.'

'Who would do a thing like that around here?' I didn't say nothing more, though, because I'd had enough from the Lightfoot boys and I couldn't prove it, anyway.

'Your Uncle Tom ...' said Aunt Anna, 'he had quite a suspicion ... I wonder if tha's right for me to tell you? ... He thought that might be you ...'

'Me!' I was very upset. It was a time for a tear to come in my eye, but I hid it. 'I wouldn't do a thing like that to you and my Uncle Tom. Why,' I said fiercely, and she could see my hands were clenched. 'I admire you too much.'

'I told him I wouldn't listen to him sayin' it. But ... well, he said he was worried about you ... well, he wouldn't say no more.'

She shook her head and then blew her nose. She went through

the whole rigmarole. Uncle Tom had heard about the injury I'd done to Tim. And then he'd seen me with the bird and the fish, and the hare. Then he was puzzled about why I kept going up that field. I decided to tell her then. I was fed up with being thought bad of. I was going to tell Aunt Anna everything. I opened my mouth to start my story when suddenly the gate crashed and there was my Uncle Tom, coming back from his walk. His face went dark when he saw me, very stern, especially as Aunt Anna and I were up the vegetable garden near where the scrumping of them apples had been done.

I didn't know what to do. So, I walked towards him, half ready to tell him everything.

'I been showing him down the garding, how those apples was taken,' said Aunt Anna.

'Ah,' said Uncle Tom, his pale, angry face fixed on me. 'I'd like to know how they went an' all.'

'I didn't take them, so you needn't think,' I said, a bit angry myself.

'I'll think what I like,' said Uncle Tom, and he shook his stick at me, not extended, but holding it downwards, striking the ground with it. 'I'm thinking a lot about you, Duffy Ransome,' he said, his moustache bristling.

Oh, he was right aggravated, and if that hadn't been for Anna he'd have walloped me there and then, I reckon.

'Now, Tom!' my old Aunt said, but he just said 'Ah!' sternly.

That was obviously no good. I went slitherin' off down the road. The chance of telling it all to my Aunt had gone, and so had my chance of taking Uncle Tom into my confidence over the torque.

EIGHTEEN

Next day a letter came from old Cave. He was sorry he hadn't replied before: he'd only just got back from holiday. It sounded very exciting what I had found in the hedge. He would very much like to come and see it, but I must realise that would take up a day, and he was very busy writing a book about Cromwell. To make sure he wouldn't be wasting his time, could I please send him a more full description of the article and if possible a drawing. Then he would go up to Norwich Castle Museum and then perhaps he would come out with an expert to look at the artefact, and the site. I had started something, hadn't I? Only now I hadn't got nothing, as they say here, to show for it.

Half of me now wanted nothing more to do with it. I was here on old Isaac's farm to recuperate, I said to myself, as I tucked in to old Mrs Walker's breakfast. She'd got me on to two eggs now in the morning and I could do with them, I was so hungry all the time. Donald and I had a nice steady job now, just sawing up a great big pile of tree limbs into logs for the winter, cutting them on a saw bench with a circular blade, driven by a belt off the tractor. Donald wouldn't let me do the cutting: I just heaved over the limbs and took away the logs to stack them in the yard. He pressed the timber against the revolving blade that sang out loudly like an organ note as the metal ripped through the wood. We got caught up in the rhythm of it and we could see this big stack of wood growing, and that looked good.

Why should I leave this job, and go and get myself into trouble with the Lightfoot boys? I didn't have any evidence; I didn't want to show them I cared about that old thing. I didn't want to get mixed up in the peevishness of a fight with those old boys. But, at the same time, I was wholly annoyed.

And then my other 'side' told me I must find that thing, for the sake of history. Why, one day, that might be a drawing in a history book! So I asked Donald for the afternoon off.

In the end I didn't have to challenge the Lightfoot boys. They couldn't contain themselves about it. I knew where they lived, in the cottages at the other end of the village where the farm workers lived. So I just went walking down past there, as if I were just exploring, but I cut myself a big stick out of the hedge, just in case.

Of course, as I expected, a sod of earth came flying over the hedge, followed by a lot of guffawing. Tim Lightfoot appeared on the bank over the hedge, calling,

'What y're doin' down here, Townee? Have you lost suffin?'

They all laughed in a jeering sort of way – and my heart leapt, because the way they laughed showed I was right. They were letting me know they had pinched my object, to get revenge on me.

'Stop chuckin' stuff or it'll get chucked back,' I shouted, trying to sound as rough as I could.

'You better not come any further down 'ere!' shouted Tim, sticking his chest out.

But the three boys had a yonker with them, a little one who was only about three. His little old face was covered in black dirt and his hair was all matted. He wanted to keep up with his brothers, but they didn't want to start anything, in case he got hurt. He tried to imitate his brothers. 'Don' come down 'ere!' he shouted.

They all laughed at him, as he picked up a stone and hurled it wildly into the air, pulling an angry face at me.

'You won't find what you're lookin' for down 'ere, Duffy Ransome,' said one of the younger ones. 'You bugger off!'

'S'right. You bugger off!' they all shouted.

''Ugger oss!' shouted the three year old. 'My bruvver 'ew it away.'

At this the Lightfoot boys, who were a bit dim, really, got the wind up. They could jeer at me and let me know they'd got my thing, but they didn't want me to have any clear evidence. They were thieves and poachers, as old Abbs said, and they'd never hand any clues to anyone, but here was the little one giving them away: as Abbs once said, 'They say a child'll 'ang you!'

The little old Lightfoot came right up to me and hurled a stone in the air, sticking his tongue out as hard as he could.

''Ugger oss!' the infant shouted. 'My bruvver frew your thing away! Frew it down the ...'

But at this point Tim jumped on him and clamped his big hand over the smutty face. The little old boy kicked and writhed, but they weren't going to let him give away any more. Tim lifted him up and tucked him under his arm, and to my surprise they all turned tail, and ran home. So I knew they'd done it. But how could I get it out of them? I couldn't fight the lot, and win, so that I could force it out of them!

NINETEEN

I woke up next day with a headache at Isaac Walker's and that seemed like something was pressing on my head, squeezing it in its big hands. I couldn't hardly lift my eyelids. I washed, and that water felt cold and nasty, and I got downstairs some old how, but I didn't want my breakfast. I ate a bit o' porridge just to please old Mrs Walker, but that seemed cold and lumpy.

That morning, I remember, old Isaac had had a kipper and that smelt really strong. Mrs Walker, she say, 'Do you mind giving them kipper bones to the dogs, Duffy?' – and that did it. I took that plate outside and was bending down to scrape that old stuff off the plate into the dogs' bowl when the full, strong smell of that smoky old fish got in my nose. The barns and the yard suddenly took off and flew round, and when I turned round old Isaac's farmhouse flew off too. My inside come heavin' right out and I ran to put my head down one of the big holes in Isaac's bumby, his two seater earth closet. That was all covered over with honeysuckle and now, whenever I'm sick, I can smell that funny old mixture of earth closet, honeysuckle, and kipper. I kept heavin' and heavin' until there wasn't nothing left in my innards.

'Oh, gawd!' I kept moanin', but poor old Mrs Walker she didn't notice me for a long time. Then she come running out with a wet cloth and wiped my face for me.

'Oh, my heart alive, he's right tidily queer sudden!'

'What's the matter with the bloody boy, now?' asked old Isaac, rather peevish, I thought, but he'd just about had enough of me. Old Tom had been tellin' him in the Bell, no doubt.

'He's ill, I reckon,' said old Mrs Walker. 'Do you go back to bed, my little old man. He look right wittery.'

So there she was again, little-old-manning me. When she took my temperature that was a hundred and one. I began to sweat. Old Mrs Walker made me some barley water, and I drank buckets and buckets of that. I filled up the little old chamber-pot she put in my room: I'd never dared use that before. I didn't want old Mrs Walker to empty that, and so I tried to sneak down with it, but then I felt seedy and nearly dropped that bugger down the stairs, so I put that back under the bed, and got back under the clothes. I was all trembly with the effort, and felt cold. I hadn't tried to eat anything.

Anyway, old Isaac got worried now and they had a long argy-bargy downstairs. The upshot was, he come to tell me, when Aunt Anna had come down for some extra milk to make some cream cheese, she had had a long talk with old Mrs Walker and they had decided I should go up there. Old Mrs Walker was willing enough to nurse me, but she had too much to do on the farm and old Anna, she persuaded her to let her do it, because I was a relative: she insisted on that. Old Mum and Dad wouldn't be back for another week.

'We'll sort that out with Ken later,' she said. 'Only if that boy's ill he want proper lookin' after.'

But Uncle Tom! Ill as I was, when I got hold of this I was really upset at the thought of being under Uncle Tom's roof, so close to him, when he thought so bad of me. By the time they moved me, in the evening, I had a temperature of a hundred and four. I just lay there, flushed and quiet. They could do what they liked. The farm-house, the stairs, the trees, the sky, all kept altering shape and going liquid, sliding about so I couldn't get them into focus. I heard someone say, 'Right! Let me just get my hand round your wrist so we can make a eujackapivvy seat ...' and smelt old Abbs' smell. Then I seemed to sail downstairs and into the Ford Saloon. Lights and shadows altered shape on the inside of the car roof. Then the whole thing happened again upwards, only this time old Abbs' face had turned into my Uncle Tom's, and to my horror it was right close to me, looking at me with its brown eyes penetrating right into me.

After that, things went very murky. I knew I was in bed, but only sometimes and partly. Faces came and went with a strange distant booming sound: they were like clouds of steam out of a kettle and the eyes and noses in them floated about, and then became the water jug and bowl on the wash-table, or the window panes. I seemed to sink into a sloppy, cold sweat and slid down a long tunnel into darkness, then the tunnel tipped up, and I was dropping down Granny Bayfield's well, down and down with that clanking music echoing round the walls. I hit the water but there was no splash, only a thicker darkness and a gurgling rushing noise. I was down there a long time, but then seemed to float up to the surface, where Aunt Anna lifted the lid of the well cover and was saying something to me.

'How are you today, my little man?'

'Little man, little man, little man!' echoed the well.

Then Uncle Tom's face come over her shoulder, looking soft and his brown eyes staring kindly at me. His moustache wasn't stiff and pointed, but soft and bushy, as if he'd just got out of bed.

'I don't think he know us,' said Tom's voice softly.

'Know us, know us,' said the boom round the well.

'Yes, I do,' said a voice which I thought was mine, and now I was trying hard to tell my Uncle and Aunt something, but though my mouth moved, the words didn't come. I could only hear the swishing of the well water, and then I slid down again into its darkness. But as I slid down I heard the voice of the little Lightfoot, the infant, shouting 'Bugger off!' and then 'threw it down the ... threw it down the ...'

Struggling to avoid being dragged into the darkness, I knew where my torque had gone. It was in the Lightfoot's well!

TWENTY

My illness went on for a couple of days, though I couldn't tell what day it was at all, except I seemed to go up and down a few times from the bottom of the well into the light. But every time I came to the top I tried harder and harder to tell my Uncle Tom, but never succeeded. Only my determination to tell him got stronger and stronger.

At last I came up and there I was with the morning light on my pillow. Only, as my will to tell got stronger, I got weaker. And at last when I stayed up, I was nearly too feeble to speak. I had had some kind of high fever and that had left me as weak as a day-old chick. I felt so weak, so hopeless now, that I was on the verge of blubbering. And old Aunt Anna, she didn't make that any better by saying, 'Oh, go you on, Tom, he's only a boy. I just don't think there's no harm in him at all.'

Uncle Tom stood there, pulling at the ends of his waxed moustache, his white collar stiff and proper, his dark eyes boring into mine.

'That boy's been a-hidin' something, and I don't suppose that'll do him or me any good if that come out, Anna. Mebbe we ought to leave him to get better a bit 'fore we have that out.'

But then he looked more kindly and a flush came into his cheeks, rather dark and stubbly cheeks, because Aunt Anna, with her face like a bright apple, had taken hold of his hand, and her eyes were all bright and trusting.

'Are you feelin' a bit better today, Duffy, boy?' he asked kindly.

So I did blubber then and broke out in a bad sob, and I even began to whine a little bit. Then I got a grip on myself and I sobbed and choked and felt horrible, hating myself for being weak and weedy, and whimpering like a little 'un. Then I got out my handkerchief and had a good blow.

'Yes,' I said, staring at his waistcoat and the watch-chain that lay across it in two big swags, with one end going down into his pocket where his big repeater watch was. He could see me looking and got that out, just like you would for a little boy, and did it now, making it chime for me.

'Ha!' said Tom, chuckling. 'You remember how I used to do that?'

Anna looked so eager, to see that he remembered me from the time when I was too young to be a bad 'un.

'Why, Tom,' she said, 'how can you think he ha' got so bad you can't speak to him.'

Tom snapped the watch to and put that away in his pocket. He became his stiff and stern self again, the steward and game warden.

'Well, he'd better speak up for himself quick now he's got the chance.'

I felt cold now and brought myself together as strongly as I could. It wasn't bringing it all out that was hard: it was the relief, of being able to get it right with old Tom that made me want to cry. So, I had that lumpy feeling in my throat and a flutter in my guts, but I managed to go on speaking, though that was ever so quiet.

'That ain't true I was ever a poacher,' I said. 'You got it all wrong about me, because of what old Abbs and Charlie Bacon said in the pub. I've never shot any game and I never fished that trout: that must have come floating down the river dead. And then that hare you saw, I released that because that had that's foot caught in a snare old Abbs and Charlie had set.'

There was a pause while I got my breath because this was it.

'I've been a bit sly … I'll tell you what … When I was working in the field below Granny Bayfield's wood, I found something in an old rabbit's hole. I didn't tell no one, but I went lookin' day after day. I found a gold ornament that's very old under the ground. Anyway, I thought that was what it was. It was all covered with muck and I couldn't be sure it was anything. But then I remembered seeing a thing like it on a school trip to the London British Museum and I thought I must have found buried treasure. Old Cave, our history master, he told us about that sort of thing and he took us there. I wrote to him about it. So, I said, I'll leave this there in the meantime but I'll tell my Uncle Tom. He run the Shell Museum and he'll know who to go to, so all this here stuff can be put in a museum, and perhaps we'll get a reward … and that won't get stolen by the Lightfoots … it were them who stole your apples … I saw 'em.'

I sank back in a very cold sweat and started to tremble. I seemed to flow away, but I was relieved and all.

'Are you a-tellin' me the truth?' said Uncle Tom, all agitated now and putting his hands in his waistcoat pocket and taking them out again, and twirling his moustache so that got more and more pointed, and sharp at the end.

'Where is this here article?'

'Oh, everything went wrong,' I cried. 'Them old boys who thought I was taking their rabbits were spying on me and then they punched me up. Old Isaac thought that was because I'd fired his gun at them, but I took the gun to show I was rabbiting not digging for treasure. I didn't want the village people to know, 'cause they'd make a mess of it. Old Abbs and Charlie made that into a good story and started winking and hinting that I was sharper nor I looked and was a poacher just like my old Dad, and that. Well, I was coming to tell you and you saw me kill the pheasant, and ever since I couldn't do nothing but what I got on the wrong side of you, Uncle Tom. I wasn't going to tell old Abbs nor Charlie because they'd have started digging that up, and sell it. And old Isaac'd have told old Mrs Isaac and she'd let it out all over …'

I couldn't go on. They understood now.

'There, Tom,' said Anna eagerly. 'Do you believe him now?'

Uncle Tom stroked his chin, thoughtfully. 'I thought, like father like son: your old Dad, I had to keep an eye on him. Ha!' he said, laughin' suddenly in his gruff way. 'That weren't very nice of me, was it? That weren't right.'

'Ah,' said old Anna, 'that was different then. In them old days them old boys had to thieve turnips out o' the field to keep alive. A rabbit, blast, that was a banquet for them … Only this boy's different. I know that. He wouldn't touch nothin' that he wasn't entitled to, certainly not in our garding … As if he'd do a wicked thing like that.' She tutted and tutted, punching up my pillow.

'What about that object, then?' I asked, weakly now.

'Where is it?' asked Tom.

'Well, that's it. The Lightfoot's took it.'

'Blast!' said Tom. 'But if there's no object to see, how do I know you're not romentin'?'

'That's what I thought you'd say,' I said. 'Only I've got a good idea where it is. I reckon the Lightfoot boys threw it down their well.'

'I'll walk up and talk to the Estate Manager about it,' said Tom. 'He'll go over with his men, like enough, straight away, only there won't be no nonsense, we'll get that up, if tha's down there. If that ain't we'll find out where them old boys put it. We'll get on to your Mr Cave and the City Museum straight away. If there's a reward, or if tha's Treasury Trove, or whether tha's old Isaac's or yours, he'll settle that accordin' to the law. Only, boy, there's no doubt the main thing is – whether tha's of any importance, historical.'

Tom drew out a red-spotted handkerchief and mopped his forehead. That done, he took my hand. That felt very weak and feeble now.

'I'm sorry, Duffy, boy: that was wrong of me, to think bad of my own nephew. Only, tha's my professional duty, do you see, to think no good of any bor at times.'

He looked really troubled and I felt sorry for him now, not afraid on him.

'Only I ought t' have give you the chance to explain, especially after what Granny Bayfield said.'

'Granny Bayfield?'

'I was up there the other day and I said to her I thought you were poaching. She say "Tom," she say, "I can see through most people, and that boy just wouldn't do it." I say, "Them young bors from Norwich'll do anything. Anyway," I say, "he've made off with a bushel of my apples." "That en't the same," she say. "You leave him alone. I bet he hain't taken them either, when you get to the heart on it!"'

'Oh, I never took nawthin!' I exclaimed, in broad Norfolk.

Old Anna was wreathed in smiles. She clasped her hands. 'Oh, that is good that's all out,' she said. 'I couldn't live with all that suspiciousness. I was so upset. Why, that poor boy, le's hope he get better and can sit in the garding, and get right well.'

'Them Lightfoot boys took the apples,' I said. 'I saw 'em a-mongeing of 'em with old Abbs and Charlie Bacon.'

'Ah,' she said. 'Anyway, that was only a bit o' ground game and a bushel o' apples. That weren't worth bringing about the end of the world for. You see,' she went on sadly, while Tom regarded her with subdued regard, 'we never had no children of our own. So we're either too soft with 'em, or too stern. And over this here business we went a bit too far the wrong way, didn't we, Tom?'

'Ah!' was all he would say, for a bit. Then he looked at me real sympathetic: I mean we really met heart to heart, stern old man that he was and me an awkward boy, really – I know that. 'Duffy,' he said, 'one of my mottoes is: "What is livin' can only die." You'll

100

understand that. You were right to keep that quiet while you thought that out and never told no one, never mind how much you suffered. Suppose someone had dug out them old relics, sold them and spent that on beer? Then perhaps that gold get melted down and then the bloke get run over – tha's all gone, along of last season's game. Look at them Lightfoots, if you're right: just chuck it down the well to spite someone. No bloody sense at all. But if them diggings is properly studied, an idea come out of that, and that'll last, even when all on us is gone.' He sat for a long time, twisting his whiskers and staring at me with his gentle brown eyes. 'There's an idea under ground up there: tha's what you're saying to me, because you couldn't say it to anyone else.'

I nodded.

Old Anna came back just then, fussin' along on her little old feet: she had been up to somethin'. She held out a little old plate and on that were four big strawberries.

'Here you are, my little man,' she said. 'They're a few of the late second crop. I know Tom wouldn't mind me a-pickin' of 'em for him. Do you eat them all up right away.'

They were real big berries, dark and glossy. She had put a little old pile of sugar alongside, for me to dip them in. My appetite that was just coming back, and them big old strawberries were lovely – they went down a real treat.

Old Tom, he sat and watched me. He wouldn't take on. Only he said to Anna, 'That old boy, he'll be spoilt by the time you finished with him: he'll get all primicky.'

'Parding?' said Anna, rather fiercely, I thought, as she plumped up my pillow for me.

TWENTY-ONE

They were lucky with the well. Old Tom had a grappling iron with spikes on for getting things out of the mill pond and the river. They put extra line on that and after half an hour's work they pulled my torque up out of the well. They were excited.

They got on the telephone to old Cave and he agreed to come down straight away. He brought a curator from Norwich Museum and two young men students in blue boiler suits; there was the Estate Manager, old Isaac because he was the tenant farmer, and my Uncle Tom and me. I led the whole party to the hedge. I was feeling a bit wobbly, but I managed to keep going. I kept looking round at all these people: it was like a dream. But old Cave, he kept close to me the other side from Tom and his face was pleased as punch. He kept saying, 'Well done, Ransome. It's evidently a genuine Anglo-Saxon ornament.'

When we got there they dug a little bit with shovels, but then there was a clink and after that they worked with little trowels and brushes. They put out a sheet to put anything on there that they found. They found another gold torque like mine all crusted up with muck, and then they didn't find nothing for a long time. That got a bit borin' standin' there so I went off for a walk up the hedge to the back, kickin' the clods in the stubble field corner where old Abbs and Charlie were putting the threshing machine together with the tractor to drive it near the stack.

'Why, blast, boy, are you better?' cried old Charlie.

'He've only got a little tissack,' cried old Abbs, wheezing. 'Wus goin' on in the hedge? What are they lookin' for? Coal?'

'No, gold,' I said. 'There's a treasure under there.'

'He's romentin' agin that bloody boy,' old Charlie cried after me.

When I came back, they had cleaned the things up a bit. There was a big twist, a bracelet or something, to wear on your arm, made of gold, too; and a big plate shaped like the moon with bits of chain, made of gold carved with a design; a couple of gold rings; and a sword handle of bronze. They were all getting excited, especially my Uncle Tom. His old whiskers were twitching like anything and his face was all pink with pleasure, his eyes lit up.

'What is it, Roman?' he said, with his gruff voice, trying to hide his excitement.

'No,' said the curator, 'this simple twist is clearly Saxon. We must study them carefully, but it looks as if it may be a Saxon burial. It's certainly a big find.'

'Worth a bit an' all, I sh'd think?' asked Tom.

I noticed old Isaac was listening very hard.

'Priceless,' said the curator man, going up on his toes. 'Priceless ... I'm not sure, of course, how it will be declared legally ... but no doubt there will be some reward for our little friend here ... and, of course, recompense for the farmer if his land is disturbed.'

Well, I had started something. Old Cave was going on at me, I hardly heard what he said.

'After this, Duffy, surely you will take history seriously? If your parents put your reward away, you could read history at a University.'

'Well,' I said, 'I'll think about it.'

I told my Uncle Tom and he nodded his old head and pulled his whiskers, and said, 'Ah, you lucky little old bor, you.' He groped after these ideas, but he didn't have the learning, he knew.

The old fellow from the museum was ever so excited, a-pokin' his nose down the burrow and lookin' all round. He said that looked as if there were a burial mound, only that had sunk over the years so you couldn't easily see the shape. He used such long words I could hardly follow him.

'Fortuitous finds like this,' he said, 'are often remarkable, because they draw attention to sites which have been completely missed by professionals. And, of course, it is most valuable to be on to the find from the beginning. You see, the importance of the find is in its relationship to the history of the whole area.'

'Ah!' said Tom, though I don't think he really took it all in.

'Well, they be a-tramplin' over my land all over then?' asked old Isaac. Evidently, he was worried.

'We would like to take measurements and surveys. Of course, you'll be compensated for any intrusion on your land and any damage, or loss of crop area. Then we shall make a thorough aerial survey: it's a new technique because we find that ancient sites invisible on the ground become visible from the air, because of differences of colour in the crops.'

'You won't want anybody diggin' at it on the off chance, any old road,' said my Uncle Tom. 'Amateurs and poachers?'

'For the time being,' said the old museum man, 'we must put some kind of guard on the site. I will get in touch with the Ministry of Works at once.'

'You might get someone out from Castle Acre,' suggested my uncle.

'When we shall be able to excavate, I couldn't say. Funds are still scarce.'

'What do they do?' I asked, feelin' a bit scared of pipin' up now that had got all official and not just my old diggin's any more.

'It's a hard, tedious, slow business,' said the curator. 'You have to do some heavy spade work at the top. But even then you've got to be careful. Then, you sit down and scrape away, an inch at a time, to ensure that nothing, however tiny, is lost. The people doing it have to watch everything – even the slight discolouration of the soil or a change in texture. You see, if the wooden haft of a spear has disappeared, it may still leave a hole, which is really a mould of its shape. If the diggers see anything like that, they stop at once ...'

'And then, when that's all laid out,' said Tom, 'you can thread your way back to their lives, and how that all was, then, hundreds of years ago. Tha's a masterpiece!'

'Yes,' said the man in his neat, grey suit, 'and I expect they would be doing just what you're doing this September – thrashing out the harvest.'

In the corner of the field old Abbs had started up the tractor, after fixing on the long belt to the thrashing machine. That clattered and roared, with its revolving screens and its chutes, shaking the corn along, and churning out the straw in a heap at the end. The barley grain came off in one sack, chaff in another, muck out of the muck spout, while the whole outfit was covered with the dust made up of the irritating blades of the barley horns.

When the little old museum man had gone off in his car with old Cave and them, to set things going into my diggings, I went up to work with old Abbs and Charlie again. We had to lift all them sheaves yet once more and put them into the big hopper on the top of the thrashing machine. And every now and then old Charlie would take a trailer full of sacks of grain over to old Isaac's barn, where we would carefully stack it. He was thunderstruck when I told him all about the discovery.

'Tha's a bloody masterpiece,' he said. 'To think them sorft buggers threw a fortune down the well!'

Old Donald, he went very funny when he heard about it.

'Silver and gold have I none,' he said, 'but such that I have give I thee … And he took him by the right hand, and lifted him up: and immediately his feet and ankle bones received strength …'

I couldn't think what he was on about.

SOME OF THE OLD NORFOLK WORDS AND
PHRASES EXPLAINED

backstock: the back of the fireplace
blah: cry (blahring is crying)
blee: to resemble
chelp: cheek
claggy: damp
clung: spoilt (used of fruit)
copping: throwing
cracking one's jaw: talking vigorously, talking too much, nagging
crawly-mawly: poorly, in poor health
crowd: push
cushies: sweets
danny: hand (used to children)
dickey: donkey
ding: a blow
discomfrontle: discomfort
dodman: a snail
duller: noise
dumpling hunter: a lay preacher who seeks to make an impression
        on people so that they ask him to dinner
duzzy: stupid, as in ' duzzy fule '
dwile: a wiping cloth
eujackapivvy: a thingamyjig
fierce: healthy
first shrugs: first pickings
foison: ripeness
foosey: gone rotten
gamarattle: nonsense
gimbling: giggling
goosegogs: gooseberries
grup: a little ditch or trench, sometimes called a gripple
hakes: hooks
half-rocked: half-mad
harns: horns (as on barley)
highlows: boots
hinderparts: hind quarters
hod-a-ma-dods: snails

hoofling: staggering
huckering: talking in a fussy way, nagging
hull: throw
hummer: a lie
imitate: try
jilk: a jerk
kicking up a stive: kicking up a dust
knackeroo: the knack, the hang of something
know something; 'he know something, don't he?':sarcastic,
    meaning he's a know-all
lampering: leaping
largers: perquisites, the harvest bonus (cf. French *largesse*)
larrikin: rowdy youth
larruping: beating
maller: mellow, ripe
masterpiece: something remarkable
mavish: thrush
mawkin: scarecrow
mawther: woman
melted: dissolved in sweat
milky doe: pregnant female rabbit
mobbing: scolding
mongeing: eating (cf. French *manger*)
muckspout: the outlet from a thrashing machine for the dirt
nonnicking: horseplay
pampling: treading delicately
parky: cold
passe: a nervous state
pightle: meadow
pishmires: ants
Pockthorpe: part of Norwich which was a slum
popple: pointless noise
primicky: hard to please
prugging about: mucking about
puckaterry: Purgatory, a torment
push: a boil or abscess
quicks: stubble
riled: upset, angry
romenting: romancing, telling lies
room of: in place of

routing: rooting
sawney: loony, soft
scalafizing: larking about
shed: used of corn when the grain falls out of the ear
shoof: sheaf
shrugs: the first portions of the spoils
shucky: untidy, dishevelled
shywanaking: shenanaking, trouble-making
slavering: talking nonsense
sluss: slush
smitticks and suslams: odd and ends
snaffle: fuss
squit: nonsense
stive: noise, trouble
swimmers: Norfolk dumplings
tankerous: cantankerous, nasty
tempest: a storm
timber hill: the stairs
tissack: a cough
twitling: whipping
tricolate: clean up
troshing: thrashing
wetshed: wetshod
wholly: ever so
whop: to hit with a stick
wittery: weak
wittles: victuals, food
yonker: a youngster

Acknowledgements

Rustic Speech and Folklore, Elizabeth Mary Wright, Oxford, 1914
Broad Norfolk, Norfolk New Co. Ltd, 1949